HEXES AND HIJINX

2

ARCANE SOULS WORLD: THE LOST WITCH

ANNIE ANDERSON

HEXES & HIJINX
ARCANE SOULS WORLD
The Lost Witch Book 2

International Bestselling Author
Annie Anderson

Print ISBN: 978-1-960315-17-5

Edited by Angela Sanders
Cover Design by Tattered Quill Designs

www.annieande.com

BOOKS BY ANNIE ANDERSON

IMMORTAL VICES & VIRTUES

HER MONSTROUS MATES

Bury Me

THE ARCANE SOULS WORLD

GRAVE TALKER SERIES

Dead to Me

Dead & Gone

Dead Calm

Dead Shift

Dead Ahead

Dead Wrong

Dead & Buried

SOUL READER SERIES

Night Watch

Death Watch

Grave Watch

THE WRONG WITCH SERIES

Spells & Slip-ups

Magic & Mayhem

Errors & Exorcisms

THE LOST WITCH SERIES

Curses & Chaos

Hexes & Hijinx

THE ETHEREAL WORLD

PHOENIX RISING SERIES

(Formerly the Ashes to Ashes Series)

Flame Kissed

Death Kissed

Fate Kissed

Shade Kissed

Sight Kissed

ROGUE ETHEREAL SERIES

Woman of Blood & Bone

Daughter of Souls & Silence

Lady of Madness & Moonlight

Sister of Embers & Echoes

Priestess of Storms & Stone

Queen of Fate & Fire

To the ones that live in the grey.

The color of truth is gray.

— ANDRÉ GIDE

CHAPTER 1
FIONA

THERE WAS NO WAY THAT JUST HAPPENED.

I mean, yes, I was there for all of it, but there was no way that in the span of the last hour and a half my life had changed so drastically that I was currently having a panic attack in Theo Acosta's bedroom. And given the state of events, said panic attack was totally warranted.

Let's see, I had been engaged to someone against my will, got attacked by my unwillingly engaged-to ex-boyfriend, watched said ex get his throat torn out by my current-ish boyfriend, got nailed against the wall next to the ex's dead body, and then totally got caught escaping from my father's compound in the middle of my engagement party. Then there was the whole declaration of war and mating to said current-ish boyfriend...

No.

No, that couldn't have all happened in that short bit of time, but... It totally had. There was way too much going on and I couldn't process any of it.

"I would really appreciate it if you got on my level," I said, pointing at Theo Acosta's face like I was brandishing a magical sword, and he would immediately start freaking out right next to me. "Why are you not freaking out?"

Or at least start pacing or *something*.

Unfortunately, Theo was Mr. Calm, Cool, and Collected, seemingly unfazed that we'd committed murder, hid a body, started a war, and got mated in less time than it took to get decent pizza. I would kill for that level of unbothered, but I'd just given my father a little finger wave while stealing a forbidden artifact and bouncing from my childhood home like it was no big deal.

I might as well have flipped him off and told him to go fuck himself at the same time.

And considering my father's declaration of war was currently carved into my arm, using a spell that I had never seen before in my fucking life, *not* freaking out wasn't exactly an option for me.

Granted, a few minutes ago, I'd been totally collected—passive, even. Ready and willing to just hand my wrist over and let Theo put his mating mark on me.

And as hot as it was, I was totally blaming shock for that one. Yeah, *shock*. But I'd just done the equivalent to a Vegas quickie wedding, only there was no annulment option once we sobered up.

This shit was permanent.

"You're freaking out enough for the both of us, Cupcake."

He wasn't wrong, but it took everything in me not to explode into a mass of bloody, fiery bits.

"Again, I need you to get on my level. And you know what's fucked up? I was about to full name you, and I don't even know if your first name is Theo or if that's short for something. What's your middle name?" I did a dramatic full-body shrug that even to me was over the top. "Who the fuck knows? I just essentially married you and I'm not sure I even know you—not really."

Theo had the unmitigated gall to smile, his full lips slicing into a gut-punch of a grin that pissed me off and made me want to rip his clothes off all at the same time. He took a seat at the edge of his bed, resting his elbows on his knees in a bad-boy, power-move pose that made that urge to rip his clothes off become almost unbearable.

A declaration of war is engraved into your skin, girl. Maybe focus on that?

Right. We needed to run for the hills. My father couldn't attack what he couldn't find, and I was the foremost expert of making powerful things disappear. Granted, the last time I'd done that, I'd ended up trapped under a null ward so strong it damn near killed me, but that was neither here nor there.

"You know me better than anyone—even my own family," he murmured, catching me by the hips on my last pacing pass and fitting me between his spread knees. "A family we should definitely fill in on this little problem before it gets worse."

Whoa, no. There was no way I was going anywhere near the Acosta pack house. "The fuck we will," I protested, backing up so fast Theo couldn't catch me. "There is absolutely no way I am walking into that house and admitting to your brother that I fucked up again. Absolutely fucking not. The city is still healing from the last time I royally screwed up, and now you want me to tell your brother that I messed up so bad my father is coming to this city? Are you high?"

I mean, I'd closed a gate to Hell that I had mistakenly opened like a day ago. There was no way I would be taking anything at all to the Acosta Alpha in the near future—maybe ever. No favors, no help, I wouldn't even ask him for the time of fucking day.

No. Just no.

I mean, yeah, it had all worked out, but not without an epic level of pain on all sides.

Theo stalked across the room, trying to corner me, but I was having none of it, snapping my fingers so the floor itself held his feet still. He just stared at the planks, dumbfounded by my magic for a solid minute before ripping his feet free, my spell unequal to Theo's determination.

"He'll understand that it wasn't our fault," he murmured, curling his arm around my waist and pulling me in. "Your father tried to sell an ABI agent to another family. The sheer fact that we just left, and you didn't arrest every single person in that compound was a fucking favor. Him taking offense to our method of exit is not enough to start a war, no matter who your daddy is."

Theo might know my father, but he didn't *know* him. He didn't know how spiteful he could be when he didn't get his way, how cruel. He didn't know the things I'd done as his enforcer, the curses I'd cast, the wrongs I was still trying to right.

But the scales were too unbalanced, and there was no way to right them.

Of course my father would sell me off—ABI agent or not. He thought he had leverage, and if there was anything Josiah Jacobs was good at, it was using whatever influence he had to come out on top.

"Why wouldn't my brother take up arms to protect

you after everything you've sacrificed for us—everything you sacrificed for him?"

Because no matter what I'd sacrificed, it wasn't enough. An entire city had been under siege because I fucked up a spell, and yeah, I fixed it, but the marks against me would never get wiped away. People lost months of their lives, the city had been crippled, the ABI had been put into chaos, magic had almost been exposed.

It wasn't just a fuck-up. It had been a damn apocalypse.

"I don't know, maybe because it's been less than forty-eight hours since I closed the gate to Hell that I accidentally opened and put the demons back in the genie bottle. How about that? No, I am getting the fuck out of here. My father can't start a war with someone he can't fucking find, and you and I both know I'm real good at hiding. I am leaving Savannah right now. You can come with me, or you can stay here. It's up to you, but I'm going."

Theo's expression darkened, his eyes glittering with the emerald green of his wolf. Cue temper tantrum in three... two... one...

"The fuck you are." His whole body seemed to double in size as hurt and rage and a fair amount of fear raced across his face. "You honestly believe that I'm going to let you go anywhere without me?"

And damn if that wouldn't be so touching if he wasn't being an overbearing asshole.

"What's this 'let' shit? You're not *letting* me do anything. I'm going before my father descends on this city like a cancer. You can come with if you want, but that doesn't change the fact that I'm fucking leaving."

Green swirled in Theo's eyes like his wolf was ready to reach across the ether and take control at any second. "You said you'd do it without me. I didn't just put my mating mark on your skin for you to ditch me. I didn't watch you wither away for months to be left behind now."

If he would have punched me in the gut, it would have hurt less. I kept forgetting that it wasn't just me down in that dungeon, day after day, month after month. Granted, back then I'd thought he hated me, so I didn't realize at the time that I'd been hurting him.

But it still didn't change the facts. We needed to get out of here, and I would not be going to the pack house. Hard. Pass. Gently, I grabbed his hand, hoping his beast was calm enough to listen.

"Then come with me. Because I am not ruining the first calm day Nico and Wren have had in years with my bullshit. I can't—I won't. My father is *my* problem."

Theo's fingers tightened on mine, pulling me into his body until I was pressed against him. "*Our* problem.

We're in this shit together, Cupcake. There's no getting rid of me now."

And damn if that didn't make me feel just a little better.

Going it alone was a daunting task, and other than Wren and the Acostas, I didn't have a whole lot of friends in the world. Sure, people liked the façade, but very few people ever saw past it. That didn't allow for a lot of people I would trust not to sell me out.

But there were a few.

By the time both of us had packed a bag, I had a general direction in mind. The transportation orb was safely buried in Forsyth Park, and I had no intention of digging it up. That meant we needed money and a mode of travel.

Well, that, and a way to move to a secure location without anyone sniffing our trail. But that would have to be done on the road. If my father knew who Theo was, then he'd know where he lived, how much money was in his bank account, and all the way down to his shoe size before dawn. If we wanted to vanish without a trace, we'd need to be smart.

I was in the middle of working out the details, when I snatched the back door open, only to stop dead in my tracks. Immediately, Theo yanked me behind him, his posture not giving an inch.

A familiar couple was standing on Theo's back porch —both tall, both blond, and both just about as deadly as two people could be. One was a Prince of Hell—not Zephyr—and the other was a woman no one wanted to be on the wrong side of. And considering I was afraid of her and not him, that said everything.

Darby Adler was the Warden of Knoxville, a shit job foisted onto her by the Arcane Council, but she made it work. She made sure the city didn't devolve into chaos and the humans never found out about the arcane side of the world.

Naturally, my father hated her with a passion.

She was also the person who'd convinced me to leave the Jacobs' life of crime and join the Arcane Bureau of Investigation. Granted, she hadn't said as much, more that she wanted better for me. We all knew how my "better" had turned out. Sure, I was still an agent, but who knew how long that would last?

"I could have sworn I told you to stay out of trouble," she chided, her blue eyes glittering with ire.

Not a good start.

"Blowing up your daddy's mansion is not my idea of keeping your nose clean, Fiona."

Wait... What?

CHAPTER 2

FIONA

"I know you," Theo growled, pointing at Aemon. "You helped Wren survive, and for that, I thank you. But I don't know you. I also don't know why you think it's appropriate to show up at my home uninvited, making wild accusations."

This time his finger was pointing at Darby, and I fought off the urge to smack him upside the head.

Darby Adler wasn't someone you pointed at—not without getting your head lopped off. "Babe, this is Darby. Darby, this is Theo. Ms. Adler is the Warden of Knoxville and a grave talker powerful enough to kill you without blinking. Maybe don't point your finger at her?"

I'd once seen her make my daddy's nose bleed just from looking at him too hard.

Plus, she was sisters with Death. And not just a

figurative "death," but the real one that reaped souls to send on to the afterlife. Word on the street was that before their father Azrael got axed, Darby was next in line for the job before it was given to her sister, but I had my doubts. I had a feeling Darby liked her job just fine as long as it wasn't trying to kill her.

Unfortunately, it was on a regular basis.

And the last time we'd seen each other, it had been while I was still working for my father. I'd like to have thought I was in a better place by now, but alas…

"Why don't you two come in?" I suggested, hoping we had enough time to get the hell out of here before shit really hit the fan. "Then you can tell me what the hell you mean by my father's house blowing up."

Theo and I backed up to allow Aemon and Darby to pass, the latter gently grabbing my chin and turning my face, her gaze locked on my lip. I ran my tongue over the spot, remembering Hendrick's brutal slap. That strike seemed like it had been years ago and not hours.

Darby's eyebrows rose as her eyes flitted from me to Theo and back. Silently, she let me know that if Theo had been the one to hit me, it would be the last thing he did on this earth.

"I'm fine," I murmured, pulling my chin out of her grip. "It wasn't him."

"Then who the fuck was it?" she demanded, her

power gathering around her like a cloak. Scuttlebutt said that Darby had been bestowed with a boatload of chaos magic, magic she still had trouble controlling from time to time.

"A man you don't have to worry about anymore," Theo answered for me as he pulled me into his side. "Now can you tell us the story already? I don't like strangers accusing my mate of shit she didn't do."

Darby's mouth spread into a smile as she looked Theo over. "Sure. But only because you asked so nicely. An explosion setting off every magical sensor the ABI has was recorded about forty-five minutes ago, coming from the Jacobs compound. By the time authorities arrived on the scene, the house was in ruins and the few survivors to be had were being pulled from the wreckage. Considering who was in that house, I will give you points for style and efficiency."

If Theo hadn't been holding me up, I would have wilted to the ground. "I-I didn't. I didn't do that. I would never."

Darby's eyebrows rose to her hairline. "So you didn't get roped into an engagement party where your father was basically selling you off to the highest bidder before storming out after telling everyone to go fuck themselves?"

"Yes, but—"

"And you didn't fireball your way through your father's guards to break into his office so you could steal one of his transportation orbs? An orb the Director of the Knoxville ABI told you to never use again because it's a forbidden, highly unstable artifact that could kill you in an instant?"

Okay, so this looks bad.

"Well, yes, but—"

Darby held up a finger, her lips pursed in a way that told me I had better shut up while I had the chance. "And then directly after that, you didn't set fire to everything in your father's safe, which bounced off all the wards in the joint and then blew that place sky high?"

Ding-ding. We have a winner.

"Everything but that last bit. I didn't set fire to anything—tough to do since we left immediately after stealing the orb. And I for damn sure didn't kill anyone."

Well, except for Hendrick, but that technically wasn't me.

But if my father volleyed a spell at me as we left, maybe it could have set the fire. "A fire like that would have immediately taken everyone out. I saw what was in that safe, it would have blown a hole in the world. Are you telling me the blast originated in my father's office? Because I call bullshit."

That would mean that the entire second floor and

anything below his office would be nothing but ash. That meant the ballroom and kitchen would be gone. That would mean my father and Paul were dead. My hand covered my mouth at the thought of Paul losing his life to my father's bullshit. Paul and I had been friends for as long as I could remember. He'd always been there looking out for me.

"Is my father among the survivors or did you find a body?" Not that there would be a body to find if he'd actually got caught up in a blast that size. Still…

Theo squeezed my hip, his reassurance needed in the middle of this. "Have you recovered his ghost? You know a man like that isn't walking into the light anytime soon."

Darby's gaze flitted to the side like she was listening to a ghost right then. She would get this far-away look in her eyes like she was talking to somebody who wasn't even there. She shook her head. "I haven't found his ghost. Unfortunately, one followed me from the wreckage, and he has been very chatty, even with his throat torn out." Exasperated, she rolled her eyes. "I get it, dude, you died. Maybe zip it for a second before I have my husband ferry your ass to Hell just to get you out of my hair."

She turned back to us. "I don't sense Josiah was killed in the blast, but the way this guy is looking at you says he might have…"

I tongued the cut on my lip. "If he looks like a frat bro with too much money and not enough sense, he's the one who slapped the shit out of me for embarrassing him. All because I wouldn't accept his proposal—only it wasn't exactly a proposal. More like an arranged marriage bargain between our parents, but whatever."

I aimed a double middle-finger salute at the open space to Darby's left. "Your death was too quick, you asshole."

A sick sort of wrath filled her expression before her gaze sliced to the ghost I still couldn't see. "You're the one who hit her? You're lucky it was him that killed you and not her. Did you have even the slightest clue as to who you were dealing with?"

Oh, he knew.

Hendrick Lane had been my boyfriend for far too long. I had a feeling our parents were involved in the courtship, however, when I'd broken up with him, my father hadn't seemed too put out about it. Granted, that was at the height of my father's power, so it made sense that he didn't care.

Too bad old Daddy couldn't hold onto the lead I'd secured for him. All he had to do was not fuck it up. *Idiot.*

Darby's hand started to glow as she latched onto something that I couldn't see. That light moved from her fingers up her arm, to her chest, then into her eyes, before she did a full-body shudder.

"Sweet baby Jesus in a manger, that boy was disgusting. Not that I would ever tell Sarina this, but you are really lucky that your man killed him when he did. As soon as y'all got married, that boy was going to slice your throat and call it good."

The growl that came from Theo was equal parts sexy as fuck and terrifying as hell. "You're right, Cupcake. I did kill him too quick."

Darby grinned like the big sister I'd never had. "He calls you 'Cupcake?' I might just perish from the cuteness. Well, I would, but I need to get you two out of here. No one knows about your involvement in the explosion—"

"I *wasn't* involved in the explosion. How many times do I have to say it? I was gone before it ever went off. And if you want a guess as to who set it," I growled, yanking up the sleeve of the flannel Theo had thrown over my shoulders, "I have a clue."

I showed her the message that was still burnt into my skin.

THIS IS WAR. YOUR WOLF CANNOT SAVE YOU FROM ME.

"If that doesn't spell Josiah Jacobs, I don't know what does."

Darby pursed her lips, staring at the message that seemed to be a permanent fixture in my flesh. "You're not lying, but that doesn't change the facts. People saw you blast your way to your father's office. Granted, they're dead and I haven't exactly said a peep, but there could be live people with the same story. It's only a matter of time before you're going to be on the ABI's shit list. We need to get out of here."

That's what I've been saying.

"I have a spot for you, a place no one in the ABI or your shithead of a father are ever going to look."

ONE GLANCE AT THE SPRAWLING CATHEDRAL IN the middle of Knoxville's arcane district, and I was absolutely positive that Darby had finally lost it.

"Are you fucking kidding me?" I hissed, staring at the Dubois nest cathedral like it would rip itself from its foundation and squash me like a bug. I did not want to be this close to Kentucky nor in the same town as a huge ABI hub.

"Is this revenge from the last time? Because honestly, I would rather you just kill me now than have to deal with whatever diabolical concoction of events you have decided to bestow upon us."

The last time Darby and I had dealt with each other, her ex was causing havoc with witches and the amount of blood magic curses floating around had been an actual problem. Granted, my daddy hadn't helped with that problem one iota, but whatever.

Darby snorted, her smile less than comforting. "Oh, come on. Don't be such a baby about it. Do you honestly believe your father is going to look for you in Tennessee of all the places you could possibly go on this plane or the next? Faerie is open again, do you really think your dad is going to be looking *here*?" she asked, gesturing at the building like she was a game show host. "Not to mention Ingrid Dubois cannot stand your father. There is no way he'd come around here poking his nose in this nest's affairs."

"She has a point," Theo whispered in my ear, hugging me close to his side like he didn't have a care in the world.

His level of unbothered still irked me, but rolling with it was my only option at this point.

Darby and Aemon led us through the wide double doors, the cathedral's interior vastly different than I'd anticipated, given the exterior. There were no pews, no lectern, but there was a dais with a sitting Queen.

Magdalena Dubois had led the Dubois nest since before the pyramids. The only older vampire I'd ever met belonged to the Night Watch and had once ruled this region beside her before I was born.

I'd met the queen once in the middle of a war, but I doubted she remembered me. But as we approached, both Magdalena and the small childlike vampire to her right stared at us with a level of stillness that had my hackles rising.

The small, blonde child was ancient—not quite as old as her queen, but close—and had terrified me from the jump.

But when she shifted her gaze to Theo, her blue eyes bleeding to red as her fangs dropped, a trill of real fear hit me. And when she launched herself at the man that was now my mate, I realized coming here was a bad idea.

Because we were well and truly *fucked*.

CHAPTER 3

THEO

ANY OTHER TIME, I MIGHT HAVE DONE THINGS different, but with my mate in the mix, there was just nothing for it.

As soon as the vampire launched herself off the dais, I knew this whole thing would go sideways if I didn't act fast. Fiona's hands sparked with magic, her fingers ready and willing to fire off something that could potentially be a bigger disaster than we were already in.

Hooking her around the waist, I tossed her to Aemon, the Prince of Hell catching her on the fly as a tiny blonde missile rocketed toward me at the speed of a freight train, knocking me to the ground like she wasn't the size of a child, but instead, a three-hundred-pound lineman hopped up on four eight-balls with a sack of bricks in his back pocket. I hit the ground hard, rolling with the ancient blonde terror until I landed flat on my ass in the middle of a vampire nest.

Good times.

Said terror smacked me on the chest before getting to her feet, her fists planted on her hips as she tapped a bedazzled tennis shoe at me like I'd just missed an appointment. "Dammit, man. You said we were going to do the *Dirty Dancing* lift the next time. You suck monkey balls, Acosta. Really, you do."

A flash of pinky-purple hair had me tensing, and when I noticed Fiona's face, I had a feeling we were one inane comment away from an explosion. Because that face said that if Aemon had not held her back, Fiona would have likely blown Ingrid to smithereens.

And maybe the whole nest.

And maybe the world.

I peeled myself off the floor. "Sorry, Ing. Maybe next time?"

Darby knocked her white braid off her shoulder as she stared at the ancient vampire. "*Dirty Dancing* lift? Really? Could you not antagonize the witch who opened up a gate to Hell, please? If she does it in Knoxville, it'll be my problem, and I have had enough of those to last until the end of time."

Shit. My eyes darted around the room, but it seemed

like this wasn't news to the horde of vampires in attendance.

Fiona pinched her brow, the exasperation hitting me square in the chest. "Does *everyone* know about that, or are you keen on spreading my business far and wide, Warden Adler?"

I'd gotten a sisterly sort of connection between Darby and my mate, but if the Warden had blabbed about the gate, I couldn't guarantee it would stay that way.

"Everyone in the room, yes," Darby affirmed, "but the ABI—at least most of them—are completely in the dark. Sarina knew as soon as it opened, but she said we couldn't change it without imploding Faerie, so..."

Sparks flew from Fiona's fingers, her blue eyes shimmering with enough power to make every vampire take a healthy step back. "Are you telling me I spent four months damn near dying for nothing? Not eating, not sleeping, wasting away, for *nothing*?"

Darby waggled her hand. "I wouldn't say nothing. Sarina said it was a fit punishment and she wouldn't go after you—or tell your boss. She said you'd know what you did, and you'd know why."

Fiona had killed thirteen witches to gain the power needed for the spell to open the gate. Granted, those people were the worst of the worst, and keeping them on the streets was such a miscarriage of justice that it made my eye twitch, but...

I supposed to the director, this was vigilantism by an active ABI agent.

To me, it was killing two birds with one stone.

Fiona and I locked eyes, and without a word, I knew we agreed on that front. Those witches were murderers, rapists, and worse. If there was any justice at all, they would have never slipped through the ABI's cracks.

"And this is why Savannah needs a Warden and the ABI needs to take a seat," Ingrid mused, crossing her arms over her chest. "If the community policed their own, then—"

Darby snorted before tucking Fiona under her arm. "You planning on leaving your nest and wrangling that city? I'll tell you, it's a shit job with not enough pay, and the benefits are garbage."

She squeezed my mate in a side-hug before turning to inspect her face again. A pale-gold glow began at her fingers, and Fiona's cut lip healed before my eyes. The bruises on her wrist and even the message burned into her skin all faded away, as if they had never been there.

"I realize this is completely pointless, but for the record, I want you to stay here, out of sight, and off the radar. No magic, no craziness, and for the love of all that is holy, please don't do anything stupid. Just stay here and be safe. Do you think you can do that for me?"

Fiona's blue eyes blazed with indignation. I knew my little spitfire of a mate hated to be told what to do—outside of the bedroom—and especially hated any sort of condescension. The Warden might as well have told her to walk into the ABI headquarters and drop trou.

"You know I didn't do this," Fiona contested, crossing her arms over her chest. "It's one thing to take out the trash. It is quite another to kill innocent people."

Darby narrowed her eyes. "I wouldn't be protecting you if I thought you did it. I wouldn't be giving you a safe place to stay or making sure that none of those ghosts blab to any other grave talkers. But some of the other guests—you know the live ones—could be flapping their gums to agents right now and then there won't be much I can do."

Fiona rolled her eyes. "So stay here and don't do anything stupid. Got it."

Darby enveloped my mate in a hug. "That's my girl. And when all this dies down, you can tell me about this 'mate' business."

With that, the Warden let Fiona go, grabbed Aemon's hand, and disappeared before our very eyes, leaving us behind.

Ingrid bumped Fiona with her hip. "Come on, Troublemaker. I'll show you two to your room."

She led us to a staircase under the pulpit that curved into a maze of catacombs, the rough stone walls smelling like they'd been freshly constructed, even though they had to be centuries old. Then again, this church had been rubble not so long ago, burnt out by a pack of wolves who had chosen the wrong path. The LeBlanc pack had turned themselves around, their new Alpha righting the ship, but the damage had been done.

"We normally keep the newbies down here until they're cured enough to not go feral, but we've had trouble recruiting after..." She trailed off, her expression darkening as she adjusted the duvet on the bed.

We'd heard about the devastation to her nest from the Battle of Knoxville. It had dwindled their numbers quite a bit, and they were still rebuilding their ranks.

The room was lush and well decorated with heavy furniture and anything we could possibly need. It even had an en suite, which seemed almost ludicrous to install in catacombs, but I supposed even newbie vamps had to use the facilities.

"Thank you for your hospitality," Fiona murmured. "We appreciate you sticking your neck out for us."

Ingrid shrugged, her blonde pigtails bouncing with the movement. "I recall a time when you stuck your neck out. Funny, I told you that you had a boon waiting for you. When all that shit in Savannah happened, why didn't you take it? We would have gotten you out, you know."

Fiona's eyebrows hit her hairline as she inspected Ingrid like she'd never seen her before. "And I thought you were kidding. I mean, yeah, we showed up to help, but anyone would have. That pack was spelled and—"

I'm sorry. What?

I must have said it aloud because both Ingrid and Fiona seemed to jump a mile in the air, both of them staring at me like I just barked that question. "Please tell me that you did not go up against an entire pack of wolves by yourself."

Fiona took a healthy step back. "A—that was three years ago. B—I didn't know you then. C—I wasn't by myself. And D—sort of? But come on, there was blood mage magic floating around, whole nests and covens and packs were getting wiped out, and I knew where the mage was sending them, so..." She threw her hands up. "An entire house full of people were getting attacked for no good reason, and I was pretty sure I was going to get blamed for it, so of course, I stepped in. That's not boon-worthy, that's just being a decent person."

Sometimes Fiona was so street smart and so naïve all at the same time. Had I known what she was like before coming to Savannah, had looked past her name to really see *her*, I probably would have gotten with the program sooner.

"I don't know a handful of people—even in my own fucking family—that would just drop everything and help some strangers just because, blood mage magic or no. But you're telling me that *you* are the witch that helped the Night Watch fend off an entire wolf pack?"

Fiona winced. "Maybe?"

I directed my attention to Ingrid, my eye practically twitching as I fought off the urge to turn Fiona over my knee and spank her ass. "Thanks. Like my mate said, we appreciate the hospitality. If ever we can return the favor, we will."

"I guess that's my cue." Ingrid shot a worried look at Fiona. "Good luck, girl. I think you're going to need it."

As soon as the vampire left, Fiona's gaze went anywhere but at me. She fiddled with the duvet, inspected the furnishings, and yet, not once did she meet my eye, not until I prowled around that bed and cornered her against the stone wall.

"So you make it a habit to help the less fortunate." It wasn't a question, and I didn't phrase it like one.

"I wouldn't call the Night Watch less fortunate. They were just going to be surrounded by wolves, compelled by a blood curse. What? Did you expect me to let them die?"

How did I explain to her that wolf wars and vampire business was absolutely, positively none of hers? I lifted her wrist to my nose, scenting the delicate skin that bore my mating mark. "Is this what I have to expect? A lifetime of you helping people get out of sticky situations?"

"You make me sound like a stuffy little do-gooder. It was for my own interests, thank you. I'd been tasked with finding the witch who'd gotten the whole curse ball rolling. If those wolves attacked the Night Watch and killed any of Darby's friends, then you know she would have blamed me for not finding the fucker that had started it. I was saving my own ass and my coven's. Excuse the fuck out of me for having an actual heart."

But this was the thing about Fiona. She never wanted to take credit for all the good things that she'd done, preferring to chastise herself, rather than believe she was worthy of a gods-be-damned "thank you." Granted, not so long ago, I hadn't been willing to give her credit either, but she had saved us more than once.

Had she gone about it the absolute wrong way? Probably, but in the end, the result was still the same. My brother was sane, the Fae gates were open, the Hell gate was gone, and Fiona had saved the day... more or less.

Yeah, we had a brand-new problem, but we'd work it out together.

I just had to keep her alive and out of trouble until then.

"You have a big heart, Cupcake. You're selfless and kind and fucking gorgeous. You know all that, right?"

Her eyes narrowed, even though her fingers fisted in my shirt. "Usually when you involve flattery, I'm about to get asked to do something I don't want to do. Please do not tell me that you want us to actually stay here," Fiona said, gesturing to the dark stone room that looked like it was straight out of a bad vampire movie.

I didn't know what the right answer was, or if we actually should stay there. All I wanted was to keep Fiona safe. Ever since I'd held her in that cell while the ABI agents were searching the pack house, that's all I ever wanted to do. I hadn't admitted it to myself then, but I'd realized not too long ago that I had been in love with Fiona Jacobs for a very long time.

"It's not that I want us to stay here, it's that I want you to think through whatever plan that is going through your beautiful head. I want you to understand that I don't care about the pack. I don't even care about me. I care about you making it through this, and the way Darby makes it sound, it feels like your father is meaning to frame you."

"You think I don't know that?" Fiona hissed, pitching her voice low so as to not let it carry through the stone tunnels. "But if I don't get out of here, if I don't get up to Kentucky and inspect that house, who knows what evidence will get trampled on? There are thousands of spells that could show me exactly what happened in that house, that could prove my innocence. And why is the ABI up in arms, anyway? You would think that with Josiah Jacobs potentially dead, they would be dancing on the tabletops."

"Didn't you say that your intended fiancé had deep connections to the ABI?"

You know, the one I killed?

Fiona's squeezed her eyes shut. "*Shit.* How much you want to bet, the Lanes think their son was lost in the blast? How much do you want to bet they are looking to pin it on my father, or me, or both. The entire coven was there, along with every crony and sycophant my father had in his back pocket. Some of them had connections, too. If they're looking for Hendrick, the Lanes aren't going to find him."

Mostly because we disposed of that body in a more... *permanent* fashion. I also wondered what would happen to all those agents once they started traipsing through the wreckage. How many scents would they destroy, how many of Josiah's wards would they trip?

"Do you honestly believe that you can do a spell that will prove what happened? That you—*we*—weren't involved?"

"Of course I do. What do you think the ABI has me do on a regular basis? Or at least they did before the Fae gates got closed and Savannah went to hell in a handbasket." She skipped toward the corridor, checking to see if the coast was clear. "Reconstructing crime scenes was my job."

And if Fiona could do that, then what else could she do?

"What do you say we get out of here, Cupcake?"

FIONA

I SORT OF FIGURED WE WOULD GET CAUGHT ON the way out of the Dubois nest. I mean, we did the smart thing and waited until almost dawn, which meant most of the vampires were in their sleeping quarters ready to bed down for the day. But I should have known Ingrid would be on high alert, waiting for us to cause mischief. Considering who I was and who she was, it wasn't exactly the biggest shock that I would jump ship.

"Come on," the little terror said, gesturing for us to follow her. Only she wasn't leading us to the catacombs underneath the cathedral or even to the front door. No, Ingrid led us to the back entrance, jingling a key fob in her small hand.

"This is Björn's. Don't scratch it, dent it, or leave it without gas, or he will figure out a way to kill me. I love

Darby, but sometimes she thinks she's the only one who knows best. Don't tell her I said so, but she's usually right, just not about this. You have to handle your family yourself. Take it from someone with a shitty family of my own, sometimes there isn't a better way. Sometimes you have to get your hands dirty. And sometimes you have to look like the bad guy for a little while until you handle your shit."

It was interesting to get such sage advice from somebody who looked like they should still be in elementary school. Granted, the number of years Ingrid had been alive boggled my mind.

"I'll drive," Theo announced, snatching the key fob from her little fingers and waltzing to the car. I would have thought he was being an ass, but he seemed to be giving Ingrid and I space.

"I still owe you, you know," she said, kicking a rock with her glittery shoe. "Your intervention saved one of my oldest and dearest friends. Hearing that they were being attacked... Had you not been there, they might not have survived. You gave them extra time. You gave them a warning, and you gave them an opportunity to call in for backup. I won't forget that. Also, this little car situation doesn't exactly make us square."

I rolled my eyes, ready to leave but she needed to understand. "Anyone would have—"

"No, kid, they wouldn't have." Ingrid's blue eyes were watery as she shook her head. "Your mate isn't kidding. There's only a handful of people in this world that would stick their neck out to save a stranger. So when you need to call in that favor—and you will—do it."

"I will," I promised, but it felt like a lie. I wasn't the one who asked for help. I was the one who passed out help like candy. Asking for help meant that you couldn't do it on your own, that you weren't good enough,

That I wasn't strong enough.

I despised my father, but that was one thing he'd given me. I would always do it myself because that was how shit got done.

"Liar," she murmured, her smile weary. "Don't worry, I'll make you take it eventually."

But I'd asked for help many times in the past, only to get shot down. The witches of Savannah refused to help me when Faerie had been sealed shut. The ABI did absolutely nothing *knowing* they had agents stuck on the other side. My father's only reason for helping anyone else was for his own benefit. I wasn't selfless. I often did things to my own benefit, but not when it came to my friends, not when it came to family, and the Acostas we're family.

I brushed my thumb over Theo's mark on my wrist. To anyone else, it would just look like I was being coy, but those indentions were a reminder that I did have a family—a brand-new, fucked-up, crazy family that I wouldn't trade for anything.

And I wouldn't let my father's bullshit touch them. Not ever.

"I know you will," I said, turning my back on Ingrid and heading for the car.

But that was a lie, too.

TWO HOURS LATER, WE WERE IN THE WOODS AT the far edge of the mountain, parked so no one would see the car from the street. If we wanted to go in undetected, we would have to hike the three miles toward the Jacobs compound, through the forest and sharp rocks and streams and bugs and who knew what else.

Yes, I had grown up in these woods, but I was an indoor girl, not an outdoor girl.

When I had said as much to Theo, he'd laughed. *I'm talking, had to lean on to the car to hold himself up, nearly rolling on the ground, laughing at me.* And all the while, I had to fight off the urge not to incinerate his fancy suit or rip a hole in one of his Italian loafers.

"You're mated to a wolf, and you don't like the outdoors?"

That mating had been a rash idea to save our asses,

not exactly a well thought out plan on my part. But whatever. He could yuck it up all he wanted.

"I'm not the one who can jump in between liminal spaces like a wizard, switching from human to animal like it's no big deal. I am going to have to *walk* those three miles in these shoes, so hush." I held up my foot to show him a flimsy ballet flat, which had been a sensible choice when I'd thought we were going to be in a city, not traipsing through the woods in the fucking mud. What would that protect me against?

Not a damn thing, that's what.

Theo still snickered as a gray mist coated his body, and then all I was left with was his animal: a wolf with emerald-green eyes that seemed to glow in the early morning light. Just like the giant wolf that once belonged to the former Acosta pack Alpha, Theo was all white, his fur pristine in a way that seemed otherworldly.

Ghost had never let me touch him, preferring to stay at Nico's side, but Theo—or Theo's wolf—was vastly different. He nearly knocked me over as he rubbed his big body against my hip, seeming to mark me with his scent. Hesitantly, I dug my fingers into the fur right behind his ears, allowing the softness to ease some of my nerves.

I didn't want to be here. I didn't want to be within a fucking mile of here. I didn't want to be within a whole-ass continent of here. But I was stuck, knowing I would need to prove my innocence, knowing somewhere in the back of my mind that my father had done this to me.

That he had betrayed his entire coven and left them to die.

That he had fucked off to save his own skin.

I *knew* it. I just had to prove it.

My heart rate had slowed, my breathing finally calmed once I knew exactly what I needed to do. Theo peeled himself from me and started walking into the tree line, letting out a little *yip* that told me to get my ass in gear.

An hour later, I was ready to kill Theo Acosta.

If human-form Theo was a mess of angst, rage, and general surliness, wolf-Theo was a—*pardon the pun*— whole other animal. In this form, Theo smelled the flowers and splashed in streams and hopped over logs like it was no big deal. He raced ahead, leaving me behind, only to double back and nudge me in the ass with his cold nose. I was fairly certain that when he finally phased back to human and fell asleep, I'd go ahead and murder him.

Yes, that seemed like the best plan.

"I swear to everything holy, if you goose my ass one more time, I'm going to hex you into oblivion," I growled, pointing at the white wolf whose fur was no longer pristine.

His paws were covered in mud and leaves were caught in his beautiful white fur. But instead of the nudge, I got the gray mist once again as Theo seemed to jump back into his human form.

"Oh, no. Don't hex me, Cupcake," Theo said with mock fright, his hands up in the air like he was ready to surrender. "I'm surprised you don't recognize these woods. Your father's compound is just through that thicket."

I didn't know how many times I needed to tell him that I was not an outdoor girl unless it was an herb garden. I didn't do dirt, and I for damn sure didn't deal with thickets or *woods*.

Theo interlaced his fingers with mine, pulling me behind him as he navigated through the trees to the clearing just beyond.

"The ABI is cleared out, but I have a feeling there are cameras. I can hear small machinery of some kind," he said, tugging on my hand to keep us from entering the space outright. "Do you think you could do something to counteract the surveillance?"

As if that wasn't the very first spell my father ever taught me.

"Of course I can." The only problem would be if

someone suspected it was me from the jump, then the surveillance would be tuned against my magic.

Only one way to find out...

A better way to do this would be to keep them intact and just turn them off and back on like no one had been there. The problem was, I was too good at my job. One of the first things that I ever ran up to my up-line boss was that surveillance equipment needed to be tamperproof to avoid the very spell that I typically would have used.

I was supposed to be on the right side of the line. Too bad it had now come to bite me in the ass.

Whispering the words I had known since I was a child, I searched out the prying eyes, and with a snap of my fingers, each one of the cameras exploded.

Theo ducked, his arm circling my middle to pull me to safety. That was until he saw the epic lack of surprise on my face.

"You could have warned a guy," Theo growled before dropping a biting kiss to my shoulder.

"Don't distract me, I have spells to work." But as soon as I broke past the tree line and discovered what was left of my father's home, I didn't know if I could do any of them.

The scent of burnt wreckage and death still permeated the air, clinging to every molecule as if it was warning us to stay away. My father's once-grand home was now mostly rubble, the centermost piece of the roof caved in, the majority of the walls charred from the fire. Both wings were burnt to ash, and it was tough for me not to be glad about that bit.

I didn't know how the council viewed retribution, but I had a feeling since Hendrick was one of their own, they wouldn't look too kindly on the Acosta Second for ripping out his throat.

The wards that had been so carefully constructed into every brick and beam, every support and even the fucking mortar we're all broken. Every bit of stored power in them gone. This was more than just an explosion—this was dark magic.

Siphoning magic.

Someone had stolen the power of this building for themselves. A normal fire, a normal bomb, would have just ruined the building's construction, but each and every piece would still be warded, those spells practically unbreakable.

"This is fucked," I murmured, gauging the energy of the broken bricks. "Someone sucked the magic out of this place."

"You can do that?"

"Oh, you sweet, summer child. That's not even half of it."

I'd done this ritual a hundred times, replaying scenes

where people had been shot or stabbed, murdered or cursed, reconstructing the reality to contradict whatever bullshit witnesses came up with. People's perspectives were usually tailored to their own wants and needs, but the replay never lied.

Hiking around the compound, I headed for the herb garden, hoping that I had a stroke of luck that Paul had managed to keep it together for me while I was gone.

Paul.

The thought of my lifelong friend being at the center of this building when it exploded made me want to vomit. I refused to think about him dying on me. I refused to believe that he was gone.

He was with Dad, and that asshole had to have skipped town or something. He had to be with my father, and that's all there was to it.

The herb garden for a coven the size of the Jacobs one had to be big, and it was. There was a large greenhouse the size of a football field down the hill filled with all sorts of plants, but this small one was mine. Surrounded by a small white picket fence, I hoped Theo didn't notice that I'd copied the one from *Practical Magic.*

We'd spent so much time in that dungeon together, watching movies, playing board games, and trying not to bite each other's heads off. He had been subjected to all of my favorites no less than a few hundred times, and if he couldn't quote the movie by now, it would be a miracle.

Finding what I needed, I rubbed the herbs together between my palms, pulling back the veil of time to show what had been just hours before. Theo helped me pick through the rubble as I held the spell in place, and as I stood at the center of the blast with the broken beams and rubble surrounding me, the magic almost convinced me that it was as if it never happened. An echo of the house's former glory seemed superimposed over reality.

Ghosts of people that had been at my engagement party waltzed through the halls and up the stairs. Guards were at their stations, caterers scurrying about. Had I not seen the destruction with my own eyes just minutes before, I would have believed the spell was the truth.

Theo and I watched ourselves run up the stairs, fight with the guards, break into my father's office. I adjusted the angle, zooming in closer, trying to see if there was something I'd missed.

Had I messed up the magic of the transportation orb?

Had I set everything on fire?

But no.

As I watched yesterday's Fiona and Theo scramble for the orb, my father stormed into his office with Paul at his side. Then yesterday's us winked out of sight, the transportation orb carrying us away on the wind. The problem with this spell was that it didn't come with audio, so I couldn't tell what curses my father was screaming when Theo and I zapped ourselves from that office and back to Savannah.

What I did know was he and Paul were perfectly fine as we left.

My father stomped across the room toward his safe, wrenching it open and capturing his own transportation orb. Dad snapped his fingers, a flame blooming from the tips as a new sort of determination drifted over his face. Paul came to his side, turning so he was just behind my father, holding on to his shoulder as my father likely whispered the words to activate the orb. Then it was as if the Paul from the past looked directly at me, as if he knew I would be here at just this moment.

He mouthed a secret word—one that only I would know, only I would see. To anyone else, this password meant nothing, but the fact that he said it was very, very bad.

"Aurora" meant that Dad was going to ground in a special hiding place, one no one knew about but him—or so he thought. A spot so warded, no one could find it—not without ten covens worth of power and a damn demon deal. No one without his blood could even enter. I didn't know what favors my father had done to get such a place, but he could be right under the ABI's nose, and they wouldn't know it.

Too bad for Dad, I'd found that spot ten years ago, while snooping through his office, and because once upon a time, I'd told Paul everything, he did, too. "Aurora" meant I knew exactly where my father was and exactly what he was doing.

As the magic of the orb closed around them both, the contents of my father's safe exploded, taking the whole house and its many inhabitants with it.

By the time the spell died, I was a sweaty, rage-filled mess, ready to tear my father apart with my bare hands.

"That lousy, no-good, double-dealing, two-faced motherfucker," I hissed, trying not to lose my mind. I whipped around, staring at Theo, the beginning of a rant on the tip of my tongue.

But while I had been watching the past like a damn soap opera, Theo had been dealing with a whole other problem.

Because when I finally followed his gaze, I realized there was a whole pack of wolves surrounding the property, surrounding us.

And they didn't look friendly.

Not.

At.

All.

CHAPTER 5

THEO

THERE WAS A SORT OF TABOO THAT CAME WITH A wolf being in another pack's territory—something I knew all about and completely disregarded when it came to Fiona. I knew being there could cause a problem, knew that even so much is stepping a toe into Knoxville or even the Kentucky region could cause strife.

And I did it, anyway.

Because when it came to Fiona, I did a lot of things I wasn't supposed to do.

So being surrounded by a pack that I'd hoped never found out that I'd been here was a wrinkle. I wasn't a fan of wrinkles. I hooked Fiona by the waist and tucked her behind me, protecting my mate in a way that let them know she was not to be touched. And as much as it galled me to do it, in the middle of the rubble of what used to be the Jacobs Coven compound, I knelt.

Would I shift to my wolf if things went sideways? Absolutely.

Did I want them to go sideways? Fuck, no, I did not. Because even with as powerful as Fiona was, I didn't know if we had enough juice to get out of there unscathed.

A gray wolf padded toward us, its silvery fur catching the morning light as his golden eyes stared us down. Quite honestly, he reminded me of my brother, his wolf similar in coloring. But I couldn't let my guard down. Letting one's guard down got people hurt, got people killed.

I'd already lost one mate to Jacobs' Coven bullshit. I wouldn't lose another one—especially not Fiona.

"We don't mean you any harm," I called, raising my hands in surrender. "My mate just wanted to visit her family's home. We apologize for stepping on your territory. We will leave this place if you allow us to."

If that Alpha read between the lines, it meant that we had ties to this land that superseded theirs, and we would leave peacefully if they didn't start shit. Considering the history of the LeBlanc pack, starting shit was their nom de plume.

The gray wolf was quickly surrounded in the mist of change, the liminal space taking over his whole form, and then he wasn't walking on four legs, but two. A tall man strode toward us, his dark skin at odds with his golden eyes.

"My niece said you wouldn't listen. She bet me fifty bucks that you'd show up here in my territory and damn the consequences. Do you know how irritating it is to always lose to that child?"

Fiona curled around me, her pink hair hanging to one side as she stared at the tall man. "Uncle Dave?" she asked, a slight giggle in her tone.

"Hey, Squirt. I could have sworn Darby told you to stay put." He looked me over.

Dave's face softened, but I was still stuck on the "Uncle Dave" bit.

"She didn't exactly give me any room to talk," Fiona grumbled. "Had she, I would have told her that I could prove my innocence with a simple spell. Unfortunately, you know how she is."

"Uncle Dave? Since when do you have an Uncle Dave that's a wolf?"

Fiona pulled me to my feet. "Before I joined the ABI there was this little battle-slash-war in Knoxville, remember? The LeBlanc pack got caught in the crossfire, and I helped track down the person who cursed them. After that, Dave LeBlanc became Uncle Dave. You know how it goes. Sometimes packs just accept you into their ranks whether you're a wolf or not."

And that little shit hadn't so much as said a peep about belonging to another pack.

"Dave, this is Theo Acosta. Theo, this is Uncle Dave."

I reached across and offered my hand, and the Alpha readily took it, his golden eyes flaring as soon as his fingers closed around mine. "An Omega. Darby didn't tell me you were dealing with an Omega, kiddo."

Pulling my hand away, I took a healthy step back. Omegas were outcasts, shunned wolves not part of any pack. "I am *not* an Omega."

Dave raised his hands in surrender. "I mean no offense, nor do I use the term as you likely know it. In recent memory, Omegas were the outcasts. I should know, I used to be one. But before the word was bastardized, it was an honorary just like Alpha or Second or Oracle. An Omega is separate but equal to an Alpha: a keeper of the peace and an enforcer of the wrath. A way to keep an Alpha from straying too far, too fast. You may carry the title, but you are no Second."

"And you ended up mating him," he continued, eyeing the silvery scar on Fiona's wrist as he shook his head. "You realize I owe Darby twice now, which means you owe me a hundred bucks, kid."

I didn't know how I felt about Dave's little revelation or if I even believed it. Omegas had been a taboo discussion for as long as I'd been alive, and I had a feeling I was more than a handful of decades older than "Uncle" Dave. Part of me loved that Fiona was ingrained in another pack, but the other part of me absolutely hated that the bond we shared was so tenuous, so new, so fragile, that the thought of losing her seemed to be burned at the forefront of my mind.

And I was more worried about losing Fiona than I ever had been about the potential of being an Omega.

"It's not my fault she has an Oracle in her back pocket. Of course she knows everything. Plus, her husband's a mind reader. It's sandbagging at best, and full-out cheating at worst. You can't blame me for that. And *stop* betting her. You know better."

Dave's smile was wide as he approached my mate, his eyes on me as he drew her close and gently pulled her into a hug. Just as gently, he set her aside, seeming to give her back to me before my wolf lost his shit.

"Come on, you two. You know Darby had a backup plan if you didn't stay with the Dubois nest. We have space for you at the house, but you're going to have to hike back through the woods to your car."

"Please tell me you're joking," Fiona grumbled, her fine-boned shoulders drooping at the thought of hiking back down the mountain.

Now that we had a whole pack with us to keep a look out, I'd probably give her a piggyback ride to save her feet.

"Of course I'm joking," Dave said, rolling his eyes as he inspected the mud on her designer flats. "Like I'd make *you* walk through the woods. What kind of monster do you take me for?"

My wince could probably be seen from space.

Fiona shot me a baleful glare. I was never going to live that one down. "As much as we appreciate the hospitality," she answered, likely mooning over the potential loss of a ride, "we can't take it. We have somewhere to be."

Dave rubbed at the stubble on his jaw, staring at Fiona like he wasn't quite sure what to do with her. "You know the agents will be back soon enough, and you better hope they don't have any shifters with them that know your scent, because it's all over this place." He sighed, stuffing his hands in his pockets. "I can't make you come with me, but I wish you would. The rumblings we hear, it's not good, kiddo. Laying low is your best option."

Fiona's smile was rueful as she shook her head. Lacing her fingers with mine, she pierced me with her gaze. I knew that look. She'd found something—something big—and we needed to get out of there and get on the road because she had a plan.

Dave seemed to sense it, too. There was no moving Fiona when she'd made up her mind. It might've been easier knocking the earth off its axis.

"Fair enough. Please at least let us give you a ride back down the mountain." He shot me a ribbing sort of grin like I would give to one of my brothers. "Only a monster would make you hike."

Fiona turned to me, sticking out her tongue. "Sure. We'll be right there. There's just one thing I need to check first."

Tugging my hand, she led me back to the center of the wreckage, her head tilted to the side like she was listening for something. She knelt, her fingers digging into the ash until she came away with a hammered gold ring.

It was nothing special, but Fiona's eyes glittered as she stared at it.

"Got you, you asshole," she muttered under her breath as she wiped the ash from the metal. She looked up at me, avarice and revenge shining in those beautiful blues. "I know where he is, and if he's not there already, he will be soon. Paul left me a message."

She stood, slipping the seemingly unassuming ring in her pocket.

"That little bastard wants to play dead? Well, how about I show him how to do it for real?"

CHAPTER 6

FIONA

I SHOULD HAVE KNOWN IT WOULD ALL COME DOWN to my father trying to save his own skin.

"Aurora" was a name for a tiny little cabin, tucked away in the Allegheny National Forest up in Pennsylvania. Coming from Kentucky, it was more than a bit of a hike, but Björn's car and Theo's lead foot made the journey quick. With the hammered gold ring practically burning a hole in my pocket, I knew my vengeance was close at hand.

That man had killed I didn't know *how* many members of his own coven and left me holding the bag. If I didn't bring his bitch ass to justice, my goose—and probably by extension, Theo's—would be cooked.

Of all the rubble and debris that made up the last

vestiges of my childhood home, nearly all of it was devoid of any sort of magic. I hadn't noticed as that spell weaved through the shell of my former home, the faint signature of power hidden under the broken beams and shattered stones. And it wasn't until I watched Paul mouth the password did I realize what that call had always been.

It was power.

Dyed in the wool, unmitigated, untamed power.

But if my father had that much juice just sitting in an easily accessible, transportable ring, why hadn't he taken it with him? Why had he siphoned all the wards, all the magic from the very stones of his home as he left, from the very people under his roof, and not taken this, too?

I spent the better part of the trip silent, as I mulled that little question over and over in my brain in the hours it took to drive from Kentucky to Pennsylvania.

But I still didn't have an answer—not one I liked, anyway.

Theo and I had stopped on the north side of Pittsburgh at a Mom-and-Pop restaurant, with a full parking lot, backed up against a whole forest of trees. One would think it would be a good idea to go to a restaurant with fewer people, but the busier the restaurant, the less likely it would be that anyone would remember us later.

And on the off chance we had a tail, it would make them easier to lose.

But the silence in the car hadn't been one-sided. I wasn't sure how well Theo had dealt with Dave's Omega pronouncement. Wolf hierarchy wasn't exactly a special interest of mine, so I didn't know what being one really entailed. What I could tell was that as soon as Dave said the big "O" word, Theo's whole body had gone on high alert.

The way he reacted, Omega was an insult. Maybe it was, but the way Dave had explained it, it seemed to fit Theo a hell of a lot more than the title "Second" ever did.

Because in the three years that Wren had been gone, Theo had been the peacemaker, the enforcer, the one who held everything together while Nico fell apart. He had made sure no one attacked us, that Savannah was safe, and all the while, still keeping an eye on me.

The insufferably gruff wolf had always made sure that I wasn't a danger to his pack, and—as much as it galled me to say it—he was damn good at his job.

Because I had been a threat. I had been in over my head. And had he not been there, I would have taken his whole pack down with me.

And now this poor bastard was mated to me to save my ass.

Again.

After peeling ourselves from the car, I headed to the bathroom while we waited for a table, the ladies' room surprisingly empty for as full as the front of the house was. I handled my business, and then went to wash my hands, happy not to be in Björn's silly sports car for the first time in hours. My ass was practically numb, the cramped bucket seats doing nothing for the long drive.

I'd just rinsed the soap off my fingers when a hand closed over my mouth and yanked me right off my feet. I caught a glimpse of a haggard Paul in the mirror before he was pulling, not toward the door, but toward the painted cinder block wall. And then we were through it, the magic wavering just a little until the small portal winked out of sight, dumping us outside in the parking lot.

"I can't believe you came here," he hissed, hitching me up his body before he tossed me over his shoulder, his long legs eating up the parking lot in the direction of the thick forest before I could even catch my breath. "You should never be this close. He'll find you. I cannot believe you came here. I mouthed 'Aurora' to tell you to stay away, you idiot."

I'd known Paul my whole life. There wasn't a day that I could remember of my time in my father's coven when he hadn't been in it. Slightly older than me, he had started out as my babysitter, then as I grew, my protector, and when I became my father's enforcer, my backup.

But right then?

It was as if he were a stranger.

And I'd had about enough of strangers calling me an idiot—especially ones that practically gave me an engraved invitation to be there. I let my knee fly, knocking into his chest as I elbowed the big idiot in the back of the head. Instead of him falling to his back like a gentleman, the dick dropped me right in the dirt, the lack of grass in this particular patch of trail making the impact ricochet up my spine and rattle my teeth.

Aces.

The only consolation was Paul landed right next to me. Unfortunately for me, the jerk just got right back up while I wheezed on the ground. Once I could finally suck in a full breath, I aimed my foot right for his shin. I didn't break the bone, but he'd have a bruise.

"Asshole," I croaked, slowly climbing to my feet as I faced off my oldest friend.

Paul rubbed his shin as he stared me down, his eyes blazing with what had to be ire, blind terror, or a little bit of both. "I thought you were smarter than this. I swear to the Fates, girl, you might as well be wearing a sign."

I could have sworn when we'd come up with the

password, it wasn't meant as a deterrent but a beacon. And I was getting tired of him calling me stupid.

"Of all the things you could pick up, why did you find that ring? And why the fuck would you keep it with you?" Paul roughly ran his fingers through his hair. "If I'd have known you would have followed us, I wouldn't have told you where we were going."

Was I on glue, or did that not make even a little bit of sense?

"What the fuck are you talking about?" I hissed through gritted teeth, closing the distance between us to jab him in the sternum with my pointer finger. "You gave me the password, telling me where you were. You did it, knowing I'd come looking once I got blamed for the blast, knowing I'd come here. And now you're pissed because I did what we'd always planned? Make it make sense, Paul."

But did Paul explain?

No. He just shook his head as he paced the edge of the parking lot like he'd lost his fucking mind. "You need to hide. Now. Do you have any idea what plan he's set in motion? You always think you know what's best, but you don't—not about this. Do you have any idea what you're carrying? Do you have any idea how easy it is to find you right now? Do you have any idea what he'll do to you if he finds out you have that ring?"

What was this, *Lord of the* fucking *Rings*?

"What are you talking about? This?" I fished the hammered gold ring out of my pocket, removing it from the pocket square Theo leant me so I wouldn't accidentally slip it on my finger. I knew better than that at least.

"Jesus, fuck. You have no idea what you're carrying. You might as well be waving a nuclear bomb in front of me."

Okay, so the power signature coming from the metal was substantial, but not worth all this drama—especially not from Paul. I covered the ring with the cloth and shoved it back into my pocket, sucking in a calming breath as I waited for Paul to make a single lick of sense.

"Anytime you want to get to the point and explain what I have, I'm all ears. Until then, could you pretty please with sugar on top try not to scare the absolute shit out of me? What's wrong with you? I mean, you couldn't have just walked up to me like a normal person? *Noooooo.* Instead, you tried to kidnap me. When Theo finds out I'm missing, you're going to get your ass kicked."

Paul's eyes widened right before a familiar streak of white knocked him to the ground, the pair of them rolling in the dirt until they disappeared in the high grass. Yes, I'd known Paul my whole life, but I couldn't stop the gust of relief that hit me, knowing Theo had taken him down.

And no, I was not going to think about why having Theo at my back made me all gooey inside. I'd examine that later. Like a lot later.

Okay, so maybe never.

"Don't kill him," I yelled, though I doubted Theo could hear me over the monstrous growl ripping up his throat. Grumbling, I snapped my fingers, knocking the two apart before they actually killed each other.

Paul huffed out a wheeze of thanks, clutching his shredded shoulder to try and stem the blood flow.

Moron.

"I didn't do it for you, dipshit," I growled, yanking wild yarrow from the ground by the roots. It would do to heal his wounds in a pinch. I rubbed it between my fingers as I gathered myself. "What were you thinking snatching me out of that restaurant? I'm mated to that big lug, you moron. You're lucky he didn't kill you."

Theo phased, standing on two feet over a bloody Paul. "I still might," he growled, his green eyes glowing with wrath. "No one touches you, Cupcake. Remember?"

Oh, I remembered all right. The last person to touch me in anger got his throat ripped out, and we were still reaping the consequences of that particular incident.

"Don't kill him," I grumbled, watching the yarrow wither to dust as Paul's wound closed, the skin as if he had never been injured at all. "He seems to have information that we need. He also seems to think we're in danger. We might want to check into that hotel we saw a few miles back and order room service instead."

Paul staggered to his feet. "I told you 'Aurora' so you knew you couldn't get in. That place is spelled so tight, you need a blood tie to get through the front fucking door. Even I couldn't get in there, and Josiah refused to take me with him. The fucker wanted me to guard the outside." Paul huffed out a mirthless laugh. "He's in a fortress, Fiona. There is no getting to him. There is no revenge. You think I don't want it, too? That blast could have killed people."

"It *did*. A lot of people." I frowned, dusting the dirt off my backside. "But I have a blood tie to bypass the wards. I'm his literal daughter. Of course I can get into that cabin, and when I do, I'm going to slit his throat and then shove his head right up his own ass."

Okay, so I probably wouldn't. I'd likely have to take the bastard alive so I could clear my name and all that, but it sure was fun to say out loud.

Paul slowly shook his head. "No, darling girl, there is no blood tie between you and Josiah Jacobs."

"What do you mean?" It sort of felt like the world was opening up beneath my feet, my gut going into free fall.

Paul's eyes flicked from Theo and then back to me, fresh guilt stamped all over his face. "Josiah Jacobs might have raised you, but you aren't his daughter. You never were."

CHAPTER 7

FIONA

"Bullshit."

Yes, that was the first thing to fall out of my mouth. No, it wasn't the most eloquent, but Paul had just dropped a verbal bomb onto my entire life, rearranging everything that I was and everything I believed myself to be.

He had to be yanking my chain, because the stain of Josiah Jacobs had been on me from the moment I'd taken my first breath. As soon as someone found out my last name, it was as if the light died in their eyes. It didn't matter if I was smart or kind or bubbly, as soon as people understood where I came from, they treated me differently.

The only person to never do that to me was Wren.

There was no way I had felt that hate—that *awful*—my whole life for it to all be a lie.

Paul's face withered, like having to tell this story was sucking the life right out of him. "There was a family that was real big in what's now our territory, some thirty-five, forty years ago, just before you were born. They had a coven bigger than anything I'd ever seen, but their hold on the region was tenuous. They had some unrest that made it so numbers were leaving their ranks en masse."

That didn't mean anything. Covens came and went. It was the way of the world.

"Your father struck up a deal to 'help' them, and by design, when this particular family couldn't pay, Josiah demanded their child as recompense. Naturally, they wouldn't give the child up, but Josiah refused to be denied. He used every single trick in the book to make their lives miserable until they paid what was due."

Yes, Dad was a hard man, but no way would he ask for a child. "That's a fairytale. You pulled that out of a Grimm's Brothers book somewhere."

But it had a ring of truth, too.

Don't kill them, Sugar Plum. No, you make them want to pay you—to only think about paying what is due. That the only way they'll be able to breathe for one more second, is to give you what you want. That's how you get ahead in this game, you always take what is owed.

Paul walked farther into the forest, resting his bones on a fallen log as he massaged his temples. "You know damn well those stories all have a bit of truth to them, because we all know that you can't go back on a deal with a Fae, or a witch, or a vampire, or a shifter. In our world, there is no such thing as not paying what's due."

Hadn't I proved that time and time again? As my father's enforcer, I made sure his deals were always followed to the letter, always paid in full.

"Your birth family, they were smart about it. They didn't want you to fall into the wrong hands, so to speak, so they bound most of your power until you came of age. But they didn't realize just how badly Josiah wanted to take over the territory—how badly he wanted to get his grubby little fingers into Kentucky, into Tennessee, into Georgia, Virginia, West Virginia. He wanted one big coven where he got to sip on every members' power until there was nothing left."

And hadn't he gotten it? The Jacobs Coven was one of the largest—or at least it had been when I'd been his enforcer.

"And he wasn't exactly happy that you were bound. Granted, he didn't notice at first. Even as powerful as you are now, he'd thought you were just like every other witch, waiting until you hit puberty for the real deal to take hold. But puberty came and went, and you were still at the same power level. So the night of your twenty-first birthday, he went back to your birth family's house, and he rounded them all up, and he cursed the flames that he'd started so they repelled water and extinguishing magic, and then he had them tied to chairs in the middle of their home, and burned them alive."

My daddy was a monster—there was no denying that. I, too, had done horrible things in service to my coven, things I didn't even want to think about. But stealing children? Cursing families? Burning people alive?

"No, he might be a lot of shitty, shitty things but Josiah Jacobs is not a kidnapper, a child stealer, a…"

Paul slowly shook his head, his eyes welling up with the worst thing of all.

Pity.

"Oh, the story gets worse. You see, they bound your power to a woman of your bloodline. It was a way to keep it safe so it never got used by him—not ever—so there was a reason he had to curse the family that way, had to kill them that way. Because the only way to lift it, the only way to unbind you, was to murder the woman who kept your magic under lock and key."

Yes, I had juice. Dad had always called me a prodigy, but… I hadn't received a big boost on my birthday or anything. Had I?

"The woman was also turning twenty-one that day,

and she looked remarkably like you. See, when Josiah went to that house that day, he almost believed you'd gotten there first—that your family stole you back. He didn't know about the twin." Paul's eyes filled with tears as he rubbed at the stubble on his jaw. "He didn't know how they'd bound you until he saw her there. Josiah went to the St. James house, rounded up the whole family, and he burned your identical twin alive."

A streak of movement broke between us, and I stumbled back.

"Say you're fucking lying," Theo growled, his hand wrapped around Paul's throat as he yanked him off that log and slammed his body into a tree. "Say it's not true. Swear to me that you're lying, and I'll fucking let you live."

Theo drew Paul close to his face before slamming him back against the tree, Paul's skull knocking into the trunk. "Was it you in that house with him? Is that why you know so much? Were you there right next to him, killing that family?"

Theo's mate—the real one, and not the one he sidled himself with—had died in a fire set by my father. He had scars covering his back from trying to pull her from the wreckage. Only a cursed flame could do that to a wolf—a flame cursed against the magic of healing, against water spells, against...

Bile rose up my throat.

I had a horrible feeling that the mate in question was the girl from Paul's story, but it couldn't be true. No way could my father kill someone that looked just like me. No way he could burn her alive. No way he could look at me every day after he'd killed her.

Tears rose in my eyes as I watched Theo wrap his hand around Paul's throat.

"Please tell me you're lying, Paul," I pleaded, wilting to the forest floor, praying that it held me up. Praying that this was all just a bad dream. But then I remembered a lifeline, a kernel of reality that buoyed my heart. "But there are pictures of Mom pregnant with me. There are pictures of her with me in the hospital. There—"

"They're fake, Fiona," he croaked, gasping for breath around Theo's grip on his airway. "It's all fake. He *stole* you."

"I don't give a shit how they fooled her," Theo growled in his face, the green of his wolf shining out of his eyes. "I want to know if you were there."

Paul tried to shake his head, but Theo's hold was just too tight. "No, it wasn't me," he choked out. "I swear."

Disgusted, Theo dropped him back to the forest floor, pacing away as he angrily speared his hands through his hair. "Then how the fuck do you know this?"

Paul rubbed his throat as he scrambled to his feet. "I wasn't there. My father was."

Paul's father had died not long after my twenty-first birthday. They'd said it was a car accident, but I'd never heard of a car accident killing one of us. Evidently, it had been a long, slow death, and Paul had been at his father's bedside when he passed.

Reality hit me like a stack of bricks.

Paul wasn't lying.

"Your dad told you on his deathbed, didn't he?" I swallowed hard, the truth the toughest of pills. "You wouldn't talk to me for weeks after that. Said you needed time. Was that so you could lie to me, to my face every day for the last fifteen years? Knowing all this, knowing my family—my real family—was dead, that I wasn't his daughter, that... Is that what you're telling me?"

Paul's long legs ate up the space between us, the big man towering over me as he pointed his sparking finger right at me.

"Your godsdamn right I lied to your face," he hissed before Theo yanked him away.

But Paul didn't go far, and his voice only got meaner. "Because the only person alive who was there that night is your father. We had a lot of deaths that summer, if you recall. It wasn't just my daddy at his side that night. It was Ethan's family, Samuel's family, all those patriarchs just dying for no good reason. And then you took my father's place as his enforcer, moving up real quick in the ranks after you got a nice big power boost on your twenty-first birthday."

Paul started pacing, rubbing at the tender skin of his throat as he shook his head. "Of course I lied to you. I kept my mouth shut, kept the secrets, because if I didn't, who's to say I wouldn't be on the slab next to my mother, my sisters, my cousins? Do you think I wouldn't lie to my best fucking friend to keep my entire family safe? You would do the same damn thing."

He was right.

I would lie, beg, borrow, and steal to keep my family safe. Hadn't I proved that in Savannah, opening that gate to Hell just to help the Acosta pack? Hadn't I done that for Wren? What was funny was I'd thought Paul was part of that family that I'd do anything for. He'd been like a brother to me.

Now, I was fighting off the urge to knock him into the next world.

"I still don't believe you," I whispered, tears filling my eyes as grains of truth started sliding into place. And even though I knew those words were a lie, I needed more than just a sordid story and a promise from a man who had lied to me day in and day out for fifteen years.

"I can prove it. That ring in your pocket? It's a St.

James annulet. Only a member of the bloodline can access that power. Josiah stole it that day from your twin's body. Kept it in his safe. Put it on your finger and you'll see I'm telling you the truth. You aren't his blood, Fi—never have been. And if you try to get into that cabin, if you try to break those wards, you'll be dead along with the rest of your family."

And as much as I wanted to believe that Paul was telling me this story to protect me, it felt like he was killing me, too. Because if he was telling me the truth, then that meant my whole life had been one big lie. It meant that my mother wasn't my mother, and my father wasn't my father, and damn it, even though they were awful, horrible people, they had been mine.

Reluctantly, I pulled the ring from my pocket, peeling back the pocket square that kept it safe.

It had called to me, the metal begging for me to hold it, to keep it, to slip it on my finger. But I knew all about cursed objects, and I was smarter than that. But now that I knew what it was, that it could prove or disprove Paul's story, it just made me want to slip it on my finger more.

Josiah stole it that day from your twin's body.

He rounded up the whole family, and he burned your identical twin alive.

Burned your twin alive.

Burned her alive.

Tears filled my eyes, blurring the ring in my hand. My gaze drifted to Theo, those glowing green eyes just about all I could make out. His mate—my twin—had died in that fire. This was her ring. And if the story were true, if Paul wasn't lying to me, if the universe really was that cruel, then this ring would prove him right.

Taking a deep breath, I slipped the ring on my finger, that faint buzzing from before hitting me in the chest like a lightning bolt. Pure power slammed into me, knocking me off my feet as it filled me up from the tips of my toes to the top of my head, I knew everything Paul said had been true.

And even though I now had more power than I knew what to do with, I'd likely just lost everything.

CHAPTER 8

THEO

I ONLY HAD SO MUCH SELF-CONTROL.

Seeing Fiona cry like that, feeling her heart break in my chest, knowing that this man had just ruined any ounce of progress I was making with this woman, made me want to rip off his head and shit down his neck.

And with each tear that fell down her face, I wanted his blood on my hands more and more. My wolf had already tasted his blood, I had his scent in my nose, and there was nowhere on this earth he could run from me. All my Cupcake would have to say was "Jump," and when it came to killing this fucker, I would gladly ask, "How high?"

I didn't know how anyone could look into her beautiful eyes day in and day out for over a decade and not want to tell her everything, and not want to make sure she knew the truth. He'd called himself her friend, and yet, he had only come out with the truth at the last possible second.

Somehow, his throat found its way into my hand again, his back slamming against a tree so hard the bark snapped. Maybe if a log fell on him, he'd get the fucking picture.

I didn't know how much I believed the story that Paul hadn't been there the night Fiona's family had been killed.

Fiona's family—her real family.

Memories of crawling through that broken burnt-out wreck of a house nearly took me over. The charred husk of my mate in my arms... Because I'd known then that my life would forever be changed. But that woman hadn't been my mate—couldn't have been—because the woman I loved was sitting there in the dirt, crying her eyes out as reality and the truth crashed over her head.

"Do you see those tears, motherfucker? You hear those sobs? Anyone on the planet would be dead for less. I don't know how much I believe your story about how you weren't there that night. You seem to know an awful lot of details for someone who heard it secondhand, but I'll give you the benefit of the doubt. I'll let you keep breathing. But please understand, you hurt her again, and you'll be dead before you hit the ground. And remember, the only reason you're still breathing, is because she'd miss you. That's it and that's all."

Paul's eyes widened, his face going purple as he clawed at my hand on his throat, begging for air. Disgusted, I let him go, his body crumpling to the forest floor like a sack of bricks.

"All I have ever done," he gasped, "was make sure that she was safe. Do you have any idea what he made her do? Do you think the rest of the coven was at her back? No, it was me. Even though my father died to keep her origins a secret, I still protected her. I still made sure she was safe. I still did my fucking job."

He turned to Fiona, who was still crying in the dirt, the magic of the ring doing nothing to dry her tears.

"You're still my best friend. You are still my family. I might have done the wrong thing, but I didn't keep that secret to hurt you. I kept the secret to save everyone else. I don't know if it was wrong or right. I don't know what right even is, but I didn't let you try to walk into that cabin. I didn't... I don't know if it will ever be enough, or if you'll forgive me for the lies I told, but you had to know you weren't his. The lives he took and the power he stole? None of it is on you."

Fiona shook her head, peeling herself from the ground as her face fell into a blank mask. Her heart was breaking, she couldn't hide that from me, but Paul didn't need to see it.

"I don't know the right answer, either. I never did. And at least you saved my life, but just like when your father died, I don't know how long it's going to take for me to look at you again."

"I figured as much. I just couldn't let you go in there. I couldn't... I'm sorry, Fi. Sorry I couldn't tell you sooner."

Then Paul picked himself up off the ground and limped toward the parking lot, Fiona's heart breaking just a little bit more with each step. She cleared her throat, dried her tears, not looking at me once before she suggested we find a hotel and bed down for the night.

By the time we made it into our hotel room, Fiona's silence, her sadness, her pain had surrounded us tight like a cocoon. Even in the dungeon, even when she was so close to death both of us could taste it, I'd never felt this much despair coming off of her. And worse. I didn't know how to fix it.

I was her mate, wasn't I? Wasn't it my job to fix heartbreak like that? Wasn't it my job to keep her from never feeling pain like this?

Wasn't it my job to give her happiness and warmth and safety? And right then she had none of that. All my beautiful mate had was silence and agony. It took everything in me not to pick her up in my arms and hold her close, but every time I reached for her, she slapped my hand away. Every time I went to speak, she shook her head. I didn't know what to do. When the door closed on our room, and she headed to the bathroom, I realized that Fiona couldn't go on like this.

Not alone.

She had to know she would never be alone, not ever. Her family might have died, she might have lost everything—probably twice now that she realized how evil the man who raised her was. But she had a family—she did. The Jacobs Coven were awful people. They took and took and took from her, but we wouldn't.

We wouldn't do that to her—not ever.

The thrum of the shower being turned on whistled through my ears, and I realized that woman would hide from me until the end of time if she could. The man who'd raised her had ripped who I thought was my mate from me, but I realized that I had to have been wrong. I'd been fooled by some cursed flames and thought the worst.

But my mate had never been in that fire. No, she was hiding from me in a hotel shower, trying to mend her own broken heart.

It took all of five seconds for me to realize I'd had about enough.

A flick of my wrist later, and the flimsy bathroom

lock was toast. Fiona gave me a startled squawk behind the glass doors of the shower, but all I did was loosen my tie and yank off my suit jacket, unbuttoning my shirt double-time.

"What are you doing? I'm showering here. Ever heard of privacy?"

"Cupcake, I have seen every single bit of you, and I'm not going to let you run away from me in this hotel room. If I wouldn't let you run for me in a dungeon or in my own home, what makes you think I'm going to let you run for me here?"

Her eyes flicked to her feet. "I'm not running from you."

"Bullshit. You're running from me because I can feel your heart breaking right here." I thumped my fist against my sternum. "I feel your worry and your pain. I feel all of it, Cupcake. Only mates do that."

She shook her head, rinsing the shampoo from her purple strands. The mirthless laugh that came out of her nearly brought me to my knees.

"It's not me," she whispered before seeming to gather herself. "I'm not your mate, Theo. It's never been me." She swallowed hard, her eyes swimming in tears before she gritted her teeth and kept right on breaking my heart. "It was her. Sure, I have her face, but I'm not her. I knew it before, but... to hear it out loud? It was different when it was some faceless stranger that my father took from you. But now that I know the truth?"

Shaking, she turned her back to me, resting her head on the tile like she was trying to keep standing.

"It was my family. He took my family from both of us. He took my sister, my twin, and he burned her alive. How am I supposed to live with the knowledge that when you look at my face, you see her instead? And the worst of it all? I don't even know what her name was. I don't know if she was funny or smart or kind. I don't know who she was at all, and still, I'm jealous of a dead girl and probably always will be."

"He fooled us—fooled me. He hid you away and kept you from me, not knowing you had a mate out there looking for you. That pull? It never goes away. The yank in my chest? I thought it was there forever, thought because she was dead, I was going to be broken until I took my last breath."

I shucked my pants and ripped open that glass door because I couldn't stand being that far apart from her anymore. She needed to be in my arms when I said this. I turned her small body, wrapping my arms around her, finally taking my first full deep breath since Paul had shattered her heart.

"It's you, Fiona. It's always been you. She couldn't have been my mate because I have always been yours and you have always been mine. Even when I hated you, even when I couldn't stand to look at your face, even when I couldn't stand to hold you in my arms, I was still yours. And a part of me thanks the universe for thrusting you into my path, because I would have missed you forever even if I didn't know you. Don't you understand? My heart belonged to you before we ever met."

She shook her head, not wanting to hear any of it. "How can you say that?"

"Easy," I said simply, the truth pouring out of me. I'd held it in so long, not wanting to admit just how much she owned me from the first time we met. "I love you. I always will. You are my mate, Fiona. You are my wife." I cupped her delicate chin, forcing her to look at me. "I love you. Do you understand me?" I tapped her sternum. "That beautiful soul, this gorgeous body, this unbelievably complicated heart. I love all of it, wouldn't trade it for anything—not even the years we spent apart."

Her lip trembled. Hell, her whole body did. "Promise?"

I lifted her up, plastering her back against the cold tile wall, enjoying the hiss that gusted from her lips as her warm body pressed against mine. "I swear to you on everything that I am and everything that I will be, on every second we share on this planet, you are mine, and I am yours, and I love you with everything I have. You're it, Fiona."

Tears tracked down her cheeks as she gave me a jerky little nod. "I believe you."

And then I couldn't help pressing my lips to hers, deepening the kiss as her happiness, her relief, her need thrummed through my veins. We hadn't had a chance to cement the bond that I'd started in my bedroom, but fuck if I was going to stop now.

Threading my fingers into her hair, I consumed her, loving every hitch of her breath and every moan. Loving how she circled her hips, seeking out my cock, wanting to be filled. A part of me wanted to hold back, to see if she would beg, but the other part wanted her searing heat surrounding me, wanted her curses, her pleas, wanted her to consume me in every possible way.

But first, I needed her "yes."

Breaking the kiss, I nipped her bottom lip with my fangs.

"I need you inside me, Theo," she moaned, her nails raking my scalp as she chased my mouth. "I need you, please."

But I needed to know I wasn't in this alone. "Tell me you feel it, too," I growled against her mouth. "Tell me you…"

But I couldn't order her to tell me she loved me. She

had to say it on her own. She had to feel it. I'd never begged before, never had the urge to want much for myself, but I wanted her more than anything. And I needed to know she...

"I love you, Theo. I thought that was a given. There's no one I'd rather fight with, no one I'd rather have as mine. I've never loved anyone the way I love you."

I couldn't quantify the relief that filled my chest as I hugged her closer to me. Letting the spray of the water wash away the fear that had filled us both, I kissed her again, devouring her mouth as I felt her magic tie us together tighter.

"Now that the pleasantries are out of the way, I want you to fuck me until I can't walk. Deal?"

If there was one thing Fiona had, it was a boatload of directness.

Notching my cock at her opening, I filled her with one smooth stroke. She'd been so confident, so demanding, but her breath still hitched, belaying her bravado.

"Be careful what you wish for, Cupcake."

And then I set out to give her whatever she asked for.

CHAPTER 9

FIONA

THE SOFT SHEETS CARESSED MY SKIN AS I reached for Theo. Finding nothing, I peeled my eyes open to see a hastily scrawled note on his pillow.

WENT TO GET BREAKFAST. DON'T BOTHER GETTING DRESSED.
    -THE HUSBAND

That was equally sexy as hell and irritating as fuck. I'd wanted to wake up next to him this time. I had only done it the once, but it reminded me of the first time I'd woken up without him by my side. That had led to an awful fight that I didn't necessarily want to think about. That train of thought, though, was a runaway one, crashing into reminders of our shared past.

But the past was dead. It was just us right then, and he was getting me breakfast—something that made my heart sing. I couldn't recall a single lover making sure I had food to eat, and Theo had always made it his personal mission to make sure I had anything I could possibly want. Honestly, if the man could hand-feed me, he would. And I'd never tell him that it was sexy as hell the way he cared for me.

Everything Theo did was sexy, the way he adjusted his tie or his cufflinks, the way he looked at the hem of my skirt or the line of my collar, the way he pulled strands of my now-pink hair just to curl it around his finger. He was always touching me, always within arm's reach, always assessing whether I was okay or not. And damn if it didn't make me love him more.

It had never been a question of whether I loved Theo Acosta. The question had always been whether or not he loved me back.

And he did.

He loved me. He cared for me. And I was his mate.

I didn't know if I necessarily believed that I'd always been what Fate had chosen for him, but damn if I wasn't willing to grab onto something good and hold onto it with all my might. Theo and the Acostas were just about the only good thing I had—the only *real* and good thing I had ever had.

No, I didn't care who I had to step on, or what I had to do, I was keeping it.

I deserved it.

I *did.*

Gently, I plucked the note from the pillow and hugged it to my chest. I loved that he left me a note, loved that he cared enough to make sure that I wasn't scared when I woke up alone. Granted, that didn't mean I was going to follow his orders.

Following orders and I weren't the best of friends.

Never had been.

I tugged on a fresh set of underwear and slipped on a silk robe, the hem landing just above mid-thigh and barely covering my ass. When he walked in that door, I was going to eat him for breakfast.

And then maybe I'd let him feed me.

I was just getting comfortable when there was an insistent knock on the hotel room door. Figuring that Theo had just left his key card by mistake, I readily opened it. Thinking back, I could pinpoint a hundred things that I had done wrong.

I should have looked through the peephole.

I should have listened to the faint niggle of doubt that screamed at the back of my brain that I was doing the wrong thing.

And I really should have put on pants.

But of course the "should haves" had not won out, because as soon as I opened that door, I realized rather quickly that the people behind it weren't Theo. A man and a woman stood on the other side of the threshold, both strangers, but they had the air of law enforcement that made me think they were likely ABI. And the pair of them caught me by surprise, just long enough for them to shove into our room and knock me on my ass.

I'd been knocked on my ass quite enough as of late, was not a fan of it, and damn if I would let it happen again.

The woman was fast, slamming her fist into my face and then my middle before I could even fire off the first spell and knocking the wind out of me faster than I could blink. I stumbled into the bed before rolling onto the ground, catching a boot in my middle from the man.

And that boot was formidable.

It knocked me from the floor into the wall, cracking the plaster as I struggled to suck in a single breath.

"Funny, she don't look so tough," the woman mused, her thick accent from up north somewhere. Maybe Boston or something? "If she weren't lighting up our locators like a damn beacon, I'd say she was an uninherit."

Uninherit. They *wished.*

"Yeah, John and Amelia told us she was going to be a problem. She don't look like a problem, does she?"

John and Amelia were Hendrick's parents—the Lanes must have sent these two chuckleheads to bring me in. I coughed, blood spattering my hand as I tried to focus. I was moving slower than usual, my coordination off.

Did they spell me before I even opened the door?

The woman latched a handcuff on my left wrist, the magical metal burning into my skin as she dragged me up. Then her fist was in my belly again, a one-two punch to my liver and ribs. On instinct, I kicked out, landing a foot to her middle, but losing my balance in the process.

But by the time I'd landed back on the floor, my rage had finally settled in, burning through any confusion spells they might have cast. Magic roiled under my skin, arching toward my fingers, begging me to fight back.

The man reared back to kick me again, but a snap of my fingers later, and his tibia was in two pieces, the audible crack of his bones breaking bringing a smile to my lips. He howled in agony before he was against the wall, my magic holding him in the air as I called the woman forth. Her feet dragged on the carpet as she fought it, but her body still sailed into my grasp, my fist closing around her throat.

And then I *squeezed*.

If I was still Josiah Jacobs enforcer, they would have been dead already. If I was still his daughter, there would be nothing left of these two assholes. But I had to think this through for once because it wasn't just me. Anything I did would blow back on more than just a wannabe mob boss with a penchant for burying bodies.

It would blow back on Theo, on the Acostas, on the life I wanted to lead that didn't have his stain on it.

I swallowed down the urge to squeeze the life out of them and started forming a plan.

"I suggest one of you two start talking before I get homicidal. Was it the Lanes that sent you?" The woman couldn't speak, but the man sure as shit could. "I suggest you answer me before I choke her to death. I'm getting blamed for several deaths already—what's one more?"

The man winced against the burn of my power holding him up. "T-they w-want to use you as leverage to find their s-son. They think Josiah k-killed him."

And while this was very beneficial for them to think, considering Theo had ripped Hendrick's throat out with his bare hands, using me as bait was kind of a dick move.

"You know damn well I didn't start that explosion. You know I have the Acosta pack and the LeBlanc pack in my corner. What kind of idiot would use me as leverage?"

"I don't know, man," he whined, his shoulders giving a truncated little shrug as the magic made him immobile. "I'm just following orders here. What was I supposed to tell them? No?"

I rolled my eyes. "Considering they aren't your superiors? Yeah."

He tried to shake his head, but barely moved. "You're so fucking new. The ABI isn't run internally. How many people do you know in the up-line management? Two? Three? Every single one of them gets their orders from somebody on the outside. It's how it's always been done. Here? Knoxville? Savannah? Phoenix? All of them are the same. It's the council, it's rich friends of friends who line pockets, who do favors. No one is above that—I don't care who you are."

Perfect. I'd traded one mob for another, only now I had a badge.

"So, the ABI knows I didn't do it."

The woman gurgled, and I marginally gave her more air. "The Lanes know you didn't do it. The ABI, though, they're getting suspicious, and the evidence isn't looking too good for you. There are witnesses that say you were blowing up the place. That kind of tends to look bad for someone like you."

Someone like me?

Did she mean a former mob princess? Did she mean

Josiah Jacobs' daughter? Just the thought of calling myself his daughter made my stomach turn. Or did she mean an ABI agent who was kind of on the outs with her employer?

All of the above?

"Do you have backup waiting for you?" I asked, using all the sweetening magic I had abandoned for so long.

It nearly made me gag, but it had to be done. I needed the truth, and they were going to give it to me one way or another. Plus, I was trying to figure out what I could do with the pair that was the least destructive and would leave no trace.

And murder was off the table.

The man's eyes drooped just slightly as he sighed, his smile turning flirtatious. "We were supposed to call in for backup," he said like he was telling me a secret. "But we decided against it. Didn't want to draw too much attention to the fact that we weren't supposed to be here."

I turned to the woman, ramping up that sweetness in such a way that she leaned into my hold on her throat, her eyelids heavy as she bit her lip. "We weren't going to hurt you," she cooed. "We just wanted to take you to the Lanes. We'd never hurt somebody like you."

It was utter horseshit, but it lent to the notion that they were on their own.

"That's good. That's real, real good. Why don't you

two crawl into bed and take a nap for me? You think you could do that?"

I let them go, and the pair walked sleepily to the bed, took off their shoes, and bedded down. One of them even started snoring in under a minute.

Okay, so maybe I'm using a little too much magic.

I didn't particularly care for this kind of power, didn't like the fact that I could make people do what I wanted against their will. With who I had grown up with, with who'd raised me, it seemed dirtier now.

Wrong.

With a few whispered words and a snap of my fingers, they were unconscious for real, not pretending like they had been just to make me happy.

I was in the middle of a memory working when Theo barged in the door, breakfast in hand.

I hadn't necessarily caught him by surprise, though. The fact he had a cup of coffee in his hand ready to strike spoke volumes.

"What the fuck?" Theo growled, stopping short when he saw the agents in our bed.

"Close the door and give me that coffee," I said, wiping the blood from my nose. "Please tell me you got pancakes or hashbrowns or something with meat in it. I'm starving."

Slack-jawed, Theo stared at the broken furniture, the

agents, and then at me. "What the fuck, Fiona? What happened?"

I dug through the bag, biting into a scalding hashbrown, chasing it with a gulp of coffee. "I'll give you two guesses, but I think you're probably only going to need one."

"They attacked you," he growled, stating the obvious.

"*Ding-ding-ding.* We have a winner. Of course they attacked me. They knocked on the door, I thought it was you, and I opened it like a moron." I held up a finger, stopping whatever he was about to say in its tracks. "Yes, I know I was wrong, don't interrupt. And they attacked. They're ABI agents. I recognize them from the Knoxville Bureau. The Lanes sent them to use me as collateral against my *daddy.*"

Just the thought of that man made me want to gag.

"Question," he rumbled, jerking the pocket square from his suit pocket, and dabbing my nose with it. "Why are they still alive?"

Oh, dear sweet mother of all that is holy. Please do not make me explain to this man why killing people left and right is a bad idea.

And *I* was the mob princess.

"Fun fact: I'm not a huge fan of murdering people. Second, disposing of dead bodies is cumbersome, tiring, and way less of a good idea than just performing a memory spell to make them forget they ever saw us here. Which is what I was doing when you walked in."

Theo plucked the coffee cup from my hand, his glowing green eyes assessing me like he was cataloging injuries to take out of their hides later.

"I'm not a fan of murdering people, either," he murmured, his thumb tracing a particularly sore spot on my cheek. "But I do it when it needs to get done. Those people put their hands on you."

My laugh was mirthless. "Oh, I'm aware," I said, wiping another stream of blood from my nose. "I was there and felt it happen. Pretty sure my septum's deviated now, but I can't kill them."

Theo's grin was ten steps past feral, his fangs growing before my eyes.

"*I* can."

"I'm sure you can, but it's harder to clean up blood spray in a place I'm not familiar with, and while, yes, I just got smacked with a boatload of power, I'm not sure that power is going to let me just kill people *willy-nilly*. So why don't you hush up, let me drink my damn coffee and let me work my magic."

Theo took a big step back, hurt coloring his face. "Are you mad I killed Hendrick?"

Oh, how to answer that question.

Was I mad that he'd taken someone's life in defense of me? No.

Did I wish he wouldn't have done it? Yes.

Because I could damn near guarantee that we wouldn't be in this situation right at this very second had he not ripped Hendrick's throat out in the middle of the guest wing of my father's estate. "I'm pretty sure we wouldn't have had to blast our way out of my father's house had you not, and I seriously doubt we'd be here right now. Am I mad? No. Do I wish things would have gone a different way? Yes."

He took another step back. "Are you blaming me?"

"For this current situation, my broken nose, or for the people I don't want to kill barging in our room to kidnap me?"

"Do you—"

I cut him off with a kiss to his angry lips. "I'm not blaming you. I am simply stating that I don't want to make the same mistake twice. If I modify their memories, they won't know we were ever here. I can remove all traces of us from this hotel, from the computer system, from everything. I can make it so they go on a wild goose chase and keep the Lanes out of our hair."

He gripped me tight to his front, almost like he couldn't make himself let me go.

"But they won't be punished for touching you."

And didn't that just make me want to melt into him. "While it's sweet that murder is your go-to, I'm going to need you to stand down on this one."

"It's not right. They shouldn't get to breathe air. They're getting off too easy."

"How about this? You find them in three to six months from now, you can kill them if you want. Just as long as it doesn't lead back to us. Deal?"

And the fact I'd just said that proved just how whacked my brain actually was. Because I *didn't* necessarily care about their lives. I cared that their deaths would lead back to us while we were on the run. How good of a person did that make me for me not to give a shit?

"Stop feeling guilty, Cupcake. They could have killed you. They gleefully waltzed into this room—not because they were following orders or doing the right thing. They were paid to hurt you, paid to kidnap you. Right?"

I gave him a hesitant nod, irritated that he could feel my guilt through the bond.

"Then they're dirty, anyway. And you can't trust a dirty agent."

But wasn't I a dirty agent, covering up my ex's death?

Hiding from the ABI? On the run, trying to take down my father? I wasn't much better than them, and I told Theo as much.

"You know better than that, Cupcake."

But I didn't know if I did.

CHAPTER 10

THEO

G RIPPING THE STEERING WHEEL, I FOUGHT THE urge to start our latest argument back up again. It wasn't that I was a bloodthirsty bastard that made me want to end the agents Fiona had memory wiped. It was that they were making me break my promise.

Letting them live, letting them go on breathing, was making me a liar.

I swore to her that no one would ever touch her, and what had they done? As soon as I left her unattended, they were on her like white on rice.

"I swear to the Fates, you're not even going to the bathroom by yourself anymore," I growled, trying not to snap the steering wheel in half.

Fiona startled in her seat, her gaze burning a hole in my cheek. "What are you talking about?"

"Let's see," I said, holding up a finger, "you go to the bathroom by yourself? You get kidnapped." I held up a second finger. "I leave you alone to go get breakfast? You almost get kidnapped. Can you see the pattern here?"

And I'd be damned if it was going to happen a third time.

"No, the pattern is I have too much power for my own good, and I can't mask for shit because I don't have the ingredients for the spell. And that's why we've been driving in circles for three fucking days trying to get to this 'cabin' that you booked for us."

I struggled to keep my eyes on the road. "But would they have tried to kidnap you if I was by your side? Riddle me that, Cupcake."

"I don't know why you're arguing with me about this," she grumbled, crossing her arms over her chest as she settled in her seat. "It's not my fault I almost got taken."

"Twice, Fiona. Twice."

Grinding my teeth, I kept my eyes on the back road that led to the cabin I'd managed to book. It was through a friend of a friend of a friend, using a burner phone and a prepaid credit card, but I'd managed it. Shit like that made me long for the days before technology when you could just skip town and not have anyone follow you. Now with computers and software and algorithms, any idiot with a search engine could drag your credit card or phone. It was exhausting.

What was worse? I had three missed calls from my brother's phone. Three missed calls from a man who shouldn't even have this number. Didn't he realize I was on the run? Was he trying to get me caught?

The argument paused for the time being, as I navigated toward our final destination, the verdant forest making my wolf ache to run free. If I wasn't so worried about some new asshole finding Fiona, I would pull off the road and run the rest of the way.

The remainder of the trip was silent, Fiona and I retreating to our separate corners as we finally found the cabin. It was a large, two-story log cabin at the foot of the Smokey Mountains, the lush tree cover and seclusion just what we needed. As soon as I opened the car door, I knew this was a good choice, the scent of pine and faint trace of human easing my nerves. No witches, no wolves, no vampires, just forest and earth and the human who had stocked the place for us.

As promised, the keys to the door were kept in a lock box so we could get in without meeting up with anyone. And since the closest neighbor was no closer than a mile away, we shouldn't see anyone at all for the entire time we were there. I breathed a little sigh of relief. This would be a good spot to hole up for a little while.

Sure, the water was from a well, and there was a septic system that we'd need to baby, but upon inspection of the kitchen, the fridge had been stocked and fresh linens had been put on the bed.

And not a single red flag hit my senses.

Fiona inspected the grounds, tossing up her magical wardings as soon as we'd parked. She wasn't as worried about the interior as I was. Evidently, if it was a step up from the ABI boot camp cabins, she didn't give a shit, her delivery informing me she was still pissed that I planned on being a tick on her ass until this shit blew over.

I watched her work from the wide wrap-around porch, my perch one of the two wooden rocking chairs. There was also a porch swing big enough for an orgy, and I amended my plans for the evening to include it. The cool mountain air was a respite from being cooped up in the car for days, and I maybe also tailored my agenda to add the giant four-poster bed in the main suite once I got my disgruntled mate to calm down a bit.

Grumbling, Fiona stomped up the porch steps, her pinky-purple hair half in her face, dirt smeared on her cheek. It had taken one healing spell to right her nose after the attack, but that didn't diminish the memory of the blood leaking from it.

Taking my life in my hands, I swept Fiona up in my

arms, crossing the threshold to the cabin like she was a brand-new bride. In a way, she was.

"What are you doing?" she asked accusingly, that perfect dark-blonde eyebrow skewering me with her fury.

I hugged her closer. "Making up. I'm tired of fighting with you. I want you safe, and sometimes I'm going to act like a territorial asshole about it. I can't promise I'll always rein it in, but I'm going to try my best." Dropping a kiss to her perfect lips, I settled onto the couch, draping her across my lap so I had access to every inch of her.

The ire in the bond melted just a bit, letting me know I was on the right track.

I was setting us up for a nice little make-out session when my cell vibrated again in my pocket. I tried to ignore it until Fiona squeaked, the phone tickling her ass as it went off yet again. I fished it out to find my brother's number flashing across the screen.

"Take a hint, little brother," I grumbled, tossing my cell on the coffee table, and returning to Fiona's lips.

Only once the phone stopped ringing, the pounding at the cabin door started.

Fiona broke the kiss, her eyes wide.

"I didn't feel anyone break the wards," she hissed, scrambling off my lap, a fireball in her hand like she was ready to go to war.

But I knew who had to be at that door—that was

confirmed a few seconds later when my brother's voice filtered through the wood.

"Please don't make me do the Alpha bullshit and command you to open this thing," Nico grumbled, his tone exasperated like *he* was the one put out.

I'd been driving for three days with an angry woman in the car, on the run in the dumbest bucket seat ever, and he was irritated? We'd traveled in circles, making sure no one was following us, trying to get everything situated, getting slapped in the face by her rage the whole time, and *he* was put out?

I ripped that door open, ready to knock my brother into next week.

Did it matter that he was rested and happy—if a little irritated? No.

Did it matter that he was all loved up and sane for the first time in three years? No.

He needed to get the hint that being here was painting a target on our backs.

"What the fuck are you doing here?"

His eyebrows hit his hairline. "I could ask you the same thing. Because you're supposed to be in Savannah with your pack. Where are you? North Carolina in the middle of some backwoods mountain retreat that isn't even on the godsdamned map. The ABI is up my ass asking where you two are, and I have to look like the asshole because I didn't fucking know. Care to share what the fuck is going on out here?"

Like his former boss wouldn't fill him in on all the gritty details and damn the consequences. "I'm sure you have all the knowledge, little brother. Why don't you tell me?"

Directly behind my brother was his mate, Wren, the redheaded witch-demon-wolf hybrid, likely the culprit of scooting past Fiona's wards without so much as an alert. Her green-gold eyes sparkled with mirth as she craned her head around me to get a glimpse of Fiona.

"Theo, can you stop holding my best friend hostage? I know you think it's for her own good, but just like the last time, it's not a good idea."

The fuck?

The "last time" she was referring to would be the four-month stint that Fiona had spent in the dungeon of the Acosta pack. Stuck under null wards she'd created, Fiona damn near died hiding from the ABI. Yes, I had kept her in that cell. Yes, every single day it made my gut twist thinking about hurting her that way. No, I would never forgive myself for what I'd had to do to keep her head attached to her shoulders.

But getting blamed for it was beyond the pale.

It took everything in me not to growl at her, took everything in me not to toss her off this porch and slam the door in her face. Wren and I had never seen eye to eye, but fuck if I would let her talk shit now.

I didn't care what kind of monster she could turn into.

But the pair of them on this doorstep did not spell good things. "I'm not holding her hostage, Wren. I'm keeping her safe. Something I have done since the beginning. And if you recall, the only reason she was in that fucking cell in the first place, was due to pulling your ass out of the fire. Maybe let's hold off on pointing fingers, shall we?"

The growl that came rumbling up her throat would give me nightmares, but if she thought she was going to waltz in here and start putting my mate down, she had another thing coming.

"What I want to know is why you didn't tell us you were having a problem?" Nico grumbled, shoving past me into the cabin. He pulled Fiona into a hug before looking her over, his nose doing that thing it did when he was scenting out a new pack member. "And you got a power boost. A big one. What the..." He trailed off, snatching up Fiona's wrist, staring at the mating mark like he'd never seen one before.

Then my brother slowly turned to me, his eyebrows at his hairline as his eyes flashed gold.

Aw, shit.

"What the fuck is this?" he demanded, showing me the mark like I hadn't been the one to put it there.

"You know what it is. It's a mating mark. Fiona is my mate."

"But how? Your mate died?"

Yep, definitely wanted to punch my brother in the face. Fiona flinched, ripping her hand out of his and stepping away, her gaze hitting the ground, and all that progress I'd made just crumbled to fucking dust.

"I know everyone says that you're the people person of our pack, but you should really learn some fucking tact if you're going to survive. Why don't you sit down and make yourself fucking comfortable since I don't see you guys leaving anytime soon."

By the time I told him all the sordid details—*more or less*—Nico had cracked open a beer and downed it in a single pull.

"You're lucky I didn't let Mom come. You think I'm inconvenient? You think I'm ruining your plans? Mom thinks everything is hunky-fucking-dory. All it'll take is one single phone call—"

"*Don't* call her. I have enough problems as it is. Fiona is lighting up like a beacon since she put on the St. James annulet. We've already been found twice. This was our chance to hole up for a little while and catch our breath. Now I don't know what we're going to do."

Wren gently took Fiona's hand, inspecting the mark in a very different way than my brother had. She seemed to be examining the magic of the bond the way Diana, our former seer, might have if she were still a member of the pack.

"It's real," she murmured, smiling at her best friend like she couldn't possibly be happier. "It's a real mating mark. See the gold cast to it? Soon, it will glow like this one." She pulled her collar aside to show Fiona her own mark. "There's no way to fake a mating mark, no way to mate someone who wasn't meant for you. The more you accept it, the faster it will cement. Do you share emotions? Feel when each other is in danger?"

The faint strain of hope on Fiona's face matched the niggle of relief she shared in the bond. "Some, but so far, it's only been me in danger. We haven't exactly talked about it," Fiona said, her tone better than the somber one she used when Nico's words had sucked the life right out of her.

And we would have talked about it, except my brother decided to barge right on in. *Asshole.*

"Yes, I feel her emotions. Yes, I feel when she is in danger. When she's apart from me, and I'm trying to get to her, I can almost see where she is. It doesn't quite feel complete yet, but it's there. But she doesn't have fangs or the super strength like you did."

Wren took her right hand, the one the St. James annulet rested on. "Unless she does, and it's being blocked somehow. You have a lot of power coming off of you, but it doesn't seem to me like you've absorbed it all. It's almost as if it's still on your skin, waiting for you to accept it."

But accepting that power meant more than just saying "yes" to it.

It meant accepting that the man who raised her had killed her family.

Had killed her sister.

And as much as Fiona knew that to be true, I didn't think she was ready to believe.

Not yet.

CHAPTER II
FIONA

NICO AND WREN SHOWING UP THERE WAS ABOUT the last thing Theo and I had wanted. But the words that had just come out of her mouth…

You have to accept it.

I loved my best friend. Considering what she and I had sacrificed for each other, it was natural for her to want to come to me in my time of need. We'd been trading that little favor back and forth for years.

But I couldn't accept the power from the ring like she said I should.

She had no idea what accepting it even meant. It meant that what Paul had said was true, without an ounce of wiggle room or explanation or good reason. It meant that everything I'd lived had been a lie. That any ounce of love the people who raised me had shown was bullshit. That everything I'd been given, every gift, every praise, every hug...

Everything had been a lie.

I didn't know how anyone was supposed to accept that and keep breathing.

"And if you can't accept it, maybe it's time you came back to the pack," Nico offered, his concern coming off of him in waves. "We can protect you both."

"You know we can't do that," I insisted, completely dumbfounded as to why they were being so pushy about this. Couldn't they understand that we were doing them a favor? "The ABI is looking for me, and I have made a mess of the pack already. You're still cleaning up Savannah because of what I did."

"Oh, for fuck's sake," Wren growled, a flash of midnight-blue scales rippling up her arm as her eyes began to glow. "You think you fucked up, but everything that went down had to happen that way. If you hadn't opened the gate to Hell, there would have been no gate for me to walk through in Faerie. If you hadn't set the demons free, we wouldn't have had an army at our disposal when the fight came to us."

She started pacing, ticking off each point on her now-clawed fingers, the sight of them making me take a huge step back. Wren's other form leaned more toward the demon dragon side than wolf, and she was more than a little terrifying.

"You didn't close the Fae gate. Tristan did. You didn't trick me into opening the damn thing. Tristan did. You didn't do anything except save an entire species worth of magic. How much of the ABI is run on Fae magic? Two-thirds, you'd say? If Faerie collapsed, what would happen to all that power? How many processes would collapse? How many people would be exposed or killed or simply fade away because that source of power was gone? Huh? Do you know?"

In fact, I did not know how much of the ABI ran on Fae magic. I assumed it wasn't much since they seemed rather reluctant to lift a fucking finger to help me when I wanted to open the gates back up, but...

"The sheer fact that everyone in our pack hasn't beaten that into your thick skull by now irritates the absolute fuck out of me."

"Don't look at me," Theo muttered. "I've been trying to beat that into her head for months now. She's just stubborn."

Wren sliced him with a look so rage-filled it was a wonder she didn't shift on the spot. But that expression softened when it cut back to me. "You didn't fuck up. You saved my godsdamned life. You even closed the Hell gate on your own, and you helped me survive Desmond's attack. I don't get why you feel like you did a bad thing. Yes, you had to hide after opening the gate—I get that—but the pack will rally around you. They always have, so I don't fucking get why you want to be on your own, doing this shit by yourselves."

I opened my mouth, but my best friend was on a roll.

"And for the love of all that is holy, we are square. I know you think you owe me huge because I went to go look for you in boot camp, and yeah, I did, but you saved me then just as much as I saved you. Because one of us kept the other from falling off the fucking mountain, and it sure as shit wasn't me."

Okay, she did have a point on that one. I'd even broken a nail during that little tumble.

"And that isn't what friendship is. It's not one of us owing the other until the end of fucking time. You saved my life. You saved our pack. You saved my husband, my mate, my heart. It isn't you who owes me, it is me who owes you. You have done nothing wrong, and we are in your debt."

Her chest heaved as she planted her fists on her hips. "And if your mate would stop kidnapping you for five seconds, carting you all over the damn country, then I would be peachy fucking keen."

I met Theo's eyes. In them I knew the truth. As true as her words were, we were still going to turn her down.

"We can't go back yet. There are people who have connections to the council, to the ABI, that sent people after me. They want to use me as collateral to draw my father out, not realizing that he could give a rat's taint about me. I can't stand the fact that Josiah is just chilling in a house somewhere, waiting for everything to blow over before he can rebuild his empire. I can't stand that he ruined everything, and for what? All because I stormed out of an engagement party I didn't agree to? It makes no fucking sense."

It felt good to call him Josiah and not "Father" or "Dad." Like accepting the truth of it all was right around the corner. I dropped my gaze to the St. James annulet, the hammered gold band carrying the weight of all my fears.

Wren marched over to the refrigerator and stole one of Theo's beers, downing it just like her husband had. "It's not vodka, but it'll do."

Crossing her arms over her chest, she stared at me for a good thirty seconds, knowing damn well I wasn't going to change my mind. "So fucking stubborn. Malia told me you would say this. She warned me that under no circumstances would you come back with us, that you would run until you figured it out yourself as you have always done your entire life. The little shit even tried to put money on it. Like I'd bet a psychic."

Malia had a big mouth and was a nosy little monster. But when she was right, she was right.

"She told me to tell you two things: one, accepting your power means accepting the bond. I didn't know what the hell she meant by that at the time, but now it makes a fuck of a lot more sense. I'm guessing that means you're going to have to take that power into yourself if you want to really be bonded to Theo, if you really want to be a St. James. Because becoming one with your real family can shed the weight of your old one."

Well, she would know, now, wouldn't she? Wren had been cursed as a child by her own mother, her own blood draining her power as the Bannister Coven sucked her dry.

"And two?" I asked, not really wanting to know what else the psychometry witch had in store for me, but accepting it all the same.

"She found a place for you to go next since we blew this cover already. A house you can go to with your real family in it." Wren passed over a folded slip of paper with an address to Whispering Waters, Georgia. "The owner of the home is the St. James Spell Keeper by the name of Jasper. She lives there with your cousins Shiloh and Poppy, and her man, Asa. Malia already called. They're expecting you."

"Are you sure about this?" I squeaked, the idea of

meeting St. James witches both absolutely thrilling and scary as hell.

Wren waggled her hand at me. "Let's say about seventy-thirty. But you have a family, Fiona—us and them. You were never a Jacobs. You don't own their sins. You never have."

THERE WAS NO WAY ON THIS EARTH—OR ANY other realm, for that matter—that I would just stroll right up to a people I didn't even know existed before today and introduce myself as a long-lost family member.

It didn't matter if they knew we were coming or not.

In fact, the only reason we were even entertaining the notion of going to Georgia at all was...

I couldn't really say. I wanted someone else to tell me Paul had been lying. That it was all bullshit and the reason I couldn't fully access the annulet's power was because I wasn't a St. James. That he'd been lying and... and...

But Paul hadn't been lying. I knew that down in my bones. He had told me the truth as he knew it, and unfortunately, he knew a fuck of a lot more truth than I did. So what did I want from these people? Proof? A shoulder to cry on? A tie to something—anything—that wasn't Josiah Jacobs?

I already had that with the Acosta pack, with Theo. I already had everything I needed, so why couldn't I accept this power as my own—why couldn't I fully believe that I was a St. James?

And why could I not fully accept myself as Theo's mate?

It was a question for the ages, that was for sure.

We'd made reservations at a local bed and breakfast from a brand-new burner phone with a brand-new prepaid credit card, the receptionist kind, if a little scatterbrained. She asked for my name three times, not remembering the alias that I'd given her until I used the sweetening magic to *make* her remember. Eventually, our room had been booked, and we made the drive back down to Georgia, bypassing Savannah entirely.

No offense to the town that had brought Theo and I together, but we wouldn't be setting one pinky toe inside the city limits until this thing blew over. I didn't care what Wren or Nico said, the pack could not house us. No one could.

Because something told me that the storm wasn't yet upon us, but it was coming.

There was no way Josiah Jacobs could just sit idly by while everything he'd built went up in smoke—even if it had been him who'd set the fire.

The burner phone vibrated in the cup holder, an

unfamiliar number flashing across the screen. Worried that it might be the bed and breakfast with a problem, I went ahead and answered it.

"Hello?"

"Stop the car," Darby ordered, her voice a bark that made me want to do what she said. Unfortunately, I wasn't the one driving.

"What? What are you talking about?"

"You're on the 341. I need you to pull off the road, and do not under any circumstances head to the bed and breakfast."

Oh, this is not good.

"How the fuck do you know about that? Do I have a tracker on my ass or something?" I covered the mouthpiece. "Pull over. Something's up."

Theo's growl vibrated through the cab as he exited the highway, rolling to a stop on the shoulder.

"There should be a dirt road about a hundred yards up ahead," Darby continued, her tinny voice just as powerful as if she were right next to me. "Pull off there, and drive about a mile."

Theo followed her directions, but the sinking feeling in my gut was there to stay.

"Your father set a trap at the B&B. I think he wants that annulet back now that he knows you can access its power."

Unless Paul told him, how would he know that? How would anyone know that? How...? "How the fuck do you know about the annulet, Darby? Is Sarina feeding you info now?"

But I didn't get an answer. Before the line clicked off, a disheveled Warden and her demon husband appeared not ten feet in front of the hood, making Theo slam on the brakes as to not hit them.

I flew out of the car. "What the fuck? Are you kidding me with this shit? Do you realize what it took to actually get here?"

Darby winced, Aemon looked completely unperturbed, and Theo hadn't stopped growling since the phone rang.

"I need you two to come over here, and not ask too many questions, because shit's about to get weird."

"Weirder than it is already?" Theo growled but circled the hood, his touch calming me slightly. "How did you know where we were?"

"Those are questions. I need you to not ask them, okay? And please know this is going to hurt me more than it hurts you—especially since you are totally going to blame me for this, but..."

Darby didn't say another word, she just crooked her finger at me, and we reluctantly followed orders. With

Theo at my back, I could almost trust that we weren't immediately going to die.

A few seconds later, Björn's beautiful sports car, the one Ingrid told me specifically not to get so much as a scratch on, the one that had served us so well over the last week, blew up. Had Theo not been at my back, I would have fallen on my ass.

"Sorry about that."

Her grip landed on my shoulder, Aemon latched onto Theo, and the four of us were yanked through space and time to land in a dungeon. A rough shove later, and Theo and I were behind bars, the cell door slamming shut before I could even react.

"I really am sorry about this, but it's for your own good. It won't be long, but it needs to happen. Deep breaths. This will all be over soon."

But all I could feel was my magic pinging off the metal bars, the null spells burning my skin as a scream worked up my throat.

I never wanted to see the inside of a cell again.

And even though Theo was with me, I wasn't sure I'd survive it.

Not this time.

CHAPTER 12
THEO

IT WAS TOUGH TO PLOT AN EFFECTIVE MURDER while your mate was crying in your arms, but somehow, some way, I would manage it. I just had to get Fiona to take one big deep breath for me, and then we'd be golden.

My poor mate had slammed her arms into the spelled bars, burning herself in the process all of once before I ended that mess. There was no way I was going to let her hurt herself—not here, not anywhere. It was bad enough we were under another null, and the ring on her finger was making the magic of this cell go full monkey shit.

"She said we wouldn't be in here for very long. Take a deep breath. You're okay, we're okay. We're in this together, Cupcake. Take a big deep breath for me." Forcing calm through the bond wasn't working, and I wasn't sure what else I could do.

And while I kept repeating my pleas, my mate curled into my arms and started crying her fucking eyes out. Granted, that was marginally better than the full-blown panic attack she'd been in the middle of just a few minutes earlier, but it was still shit.

"Someone had better come down here and explain some shit to us. These bars don't burn me like they burn her," I called, the view not allowing me to know whether or not we were alone down here. But my voice was loud enough that if someone could hear us, they damn well would.

"Why would she do this? Why would she lock me up? I didn't kill those people. I didn't—"

That, I didn't know, but I had to have some form of faith, even if I didn't believe it. Because Fiona needed me to be strong for her, she did. It was bad enough that there was more panic flooding our connection than I'd ever felt coming off of her before, but the fact that we now knew that the ring muted most of our connection, Fiona was about three steps away from full-blown insanity.

"She thinks she's doing the right thing, Cupcake. Let's hope she's right and it really is just a few minutes."

But Fiona's breath never slowed, her whole body trembling in my arms. Yep. I would murder someone... just as soon as I figured out how to end a damn demigod.

In the meantime, I would have to pull out the big

guns to keep Fiona calm before I devised a plan to break us out of this cell from the inside. While I planned, I started humming a tune I knew well enough. I'd heard it on the radio a few times, and the register was deep enough that my voice wouldn't break while I sang it. I wasn't a big singer. I didn't like to draw attention to myself at all, but Fiona needed me and there were plenty of times that I had hummed a tune or two in the Acosta dungeon, though usually she was unconscious when I did it.

Eventually, we started rocking together, my ass planted on the rather comfortable cot, hugging my mate to my chest as we settled in to wait. By the time the song was done, I'd moved on to another tune, keeping the soundtrack rolling as Fiona's fear knocked down notch by notch, bit by bit, until she fell into a fitful sleep against my chest.

A flash of white had me focusing on a guilty Darby with her hands in her pockets. She settled onto a metal folding chair as she looked on, whatever explanation she had not worthy of Fiona's tears. I didn't react, didn't allow my rage to fill our connection. I simply stared at the Warden of Knoxville, my face doing all the talking.

"They're almost done upstairs, and then she'll have an amulet to wear that will hide her from Josiah. I didn't want to do this, I swear, but if we didn't get her into a null cell and quick, they were going to find her here, too."

"You could have explained that to her," I murmured, fighting every instinct I had to start yelling. "Do you have any idea what it's like for her to be locked up?"

Darby rested her head on the cinder block wall. "I sure do. I spent a year in an ABI prison. I don't like it either, and fun fact: I liked being in tunnels even less. I know all about PTSD, and while it is made of suck ass, we make sacrifices when shit needs to get done. If I had explained it to her, she would have waited. They would have found her. At least I shoved you in there with her—not that it makes me feel any better."

"Well, boo-hoo for you. Everybody's got a reason for something, don't they? A justification for hurting the people they love. It's fucking bullshit, you know that?"

Darby nodded, guilt suffusing her face.

"Yep, it is bullshit. I could have handled it better, could have been kinder. Then again, maybe I couldn't have. I was an asshole, and I don't particularly like being the asshole. Hopefully, one day she'll forgive me, especially when she knows why. I know better than to ask you for that. If you'd have done the same thing to me, I doubt I would be so forgiving."

"Well, at least you're self-aware. I'll give you that. Want to tell me what's going on here?"

She leaned forward, resting her elbows on her knees. "Not particularly. I want to tell her, and it's not something I necessarily want to do twice." She swallowed hard, her eyes misting over. "I know what it's like to get betrayed by someone you thought loved you. I've been in those shoes, and I'm not real proud that I'm the one who made her wear them."

"You've got to give me something more than a bullshit apology and some vague answers. Would you accept that about your own mate? Or do you not give a shit about his feelings, either?"

"Fine," she murmured, sitting back in the chair. "The bed and breakfast was a trap. Someone had already sussed out where other St. James witches were. They tried to attack Jasper's home, not realizing that she had a ghoul and a formidable Fae on the property. Josiah's men didn't make it, but we realized that you two were being followed. We couldn't figure out what it was that had you tracked. The annulet is a beacon, yes, but only if you're of the bloodline, so it had to be another way."

"So you thought it was our clothes? The car? Our phones? What?"

Darby shrugged. "We still don't know. That's why you're in a null cell while we figure it out."

"How could they have put a tracker on her—on us?"

But it wasn't us. It was her, and who had touched her? Picked her up? Tried to kidnap her?

"Fucking Paul. He tried to kidnap her in Pennsylvania, took her right out of the restaurant bathroom, nearly exposed his magic to humans as he did it. He said he was following the ring, but he was following her, wasn't he?"

"It's possible that when he touched her skin, he put a tracking spell on her. Whether or not he did it of his own free will is a whole other matter. Fiona is an expert at sweetening magic. Who do you think she learned that from? You don't think he got to where he is today on his own, do you?"

Fiona sniffled in my arms, snuggling closer, but her eyes remained shut and her breaths even.

"If that were true, then why is everything falling apart with Fiona gone? I heard plenty about that asshole even from Savannah, but the bonds surrounding him? He couldn't beg those people to do his bidding now. Not that it matters since most of them are dead, but..."

Darby winced. "It could be because he drained the wards, giving him a power boost. It could be desperation. I don't know."

I swallowed hard, knowing that the worst was yet to come. "If Paul is the reason she's getting attacked, it's going to break her heart. You realize that, right?"

She nodded. "I met Paul a couple years back. He really cared about her like she was family. I don't think he'd do anything to hurt her of his own free will."

But it didn't matter if Paul had done it on his own or if he was directed by the whack job who raised Fiona. The damage was still done. We were still in this cell. Fiona was still trapped, and we still knew nothing about how to make this end.

"Why don't you see what the holdup is? I don't want her to wake up and still be in this cell."

Darby looked Fiona over, seeming to contemplate just what she had done, just how much damage that one act alone had wrought. Without a word, she stood from the chair, the legs scraping a bit on the cement floor, and she marched out of sight. The heavy *thud* of a metal door closing rumbled through the space. I clutched Fiona closer to my chest, settling in, knowing this was going to take far longer than any of us wanted it to.

"Is she really gone?" Fiona whispered, the eye closest to my chest peeking open while the rest of her face was a mask of feigned sleep.

"Yes, you little faker. How much of that did you hear?"

Fiona shrugged, her fingers playing with the knot of my tie. "All of it. I was never asleep, though your singing did calm me down. I didn't know you were a Cigarettes After Sex kind of guy. I'll have to remember that."

I rolled my eyes, ignoring her jab. So I listened to recent music. I was old, not dead.

"You feeling better?" I asked, knowing the answer but needing her response, anyway.

Her gaze drifted from my chest back to the bars. "Nope, but I am calmer. I liked your voice. I used to listen to it back at the pack house. You would hum and sing under your breath when you were bored. It was fine entertainment."

I fought off the urge to smack her ass. "You were supposed to be sleeping."

"I'm a good actress, but those nights when you would sing to me, those were some of the best nights I ever had down there. Other than, you know, getting absolutely wrecked at *Clue*. You couldn't let me win, like ever?"

"Absolutely not. How will you learn?"

I tugged her close, flipping us so she was underneath me. If she needed a distraction, I damn well could give it to her. I couldn't have done this before with her stuck on the inside and me on the out, but I'd come to realize over the past week, I'd rather be by Fiona's side than anywhere else on the planet.

Fiona fisted her fingers in the lapel of my jacket, tugging me closer, when we heard a throat clearing on the other side of those bars. Reluctantly, we broke apart. A small woman with golden skin and a mass of braids was on the other side of the bars, a silver necklace in her hand.

"Sorry to interrupt," the woman said, a smile curving her lips like she wasn't necessarily apologetic at all.

"Dahlia?" Fiona asked, pushing me aside so she could sit up. "Am I at the Night Watch? What the shit? Why would they bring me back to Knoxville?"

"I'll fill you in when we get upstairs. Would you like your 'Get out of Jail Free' card or not?" Dahlia asked, jingling the necklace, its glowing violet pendant swinging to and fro.

"Gimme," Fiona ordered, scrambling off the cot, her hands outstretched, practically begging to get out of the cell.

A *swish* of the doors later, and Fiona had that amulet around the delicate column of her neck.

"Now, let's get the hell out of here," Dahlia offered, pointing to a giant metal door up a set of stone steps.

"It's time to meet your real family."

CHAPTER 13
FIONA

THIS WASN'T THE FIRST TIME THAT I HAD BEEN inside the Night Watch house, but it had been the first time I'd been able to actually inspect the home. Following Dahlia up the stone stairs, she yanked open the metal door after a set of complicated hand gestures that had to have been a mage lock. Only then did we follow her into a large sitting room, filled with dark wood moldings and wall-to-wall bookshelves.

Plush chairs and couches were scattered throughout the space as if someone—*or several someones*—just had to curl up in one of them and read a book at any given second of the day. A grand staircase on my left led to a giant balcony, the thick newel post topped with a falcon, its wings spread wide. It had my eyes traveling up to the high vaulted ceilings and wide windows, the night falling in earnest.

But the sitting room wasn't empty, the chairs filled with four women, with Dahlia taking the fifth seat. I knew Darby and Dahlia, but the rest…?

A tall, willowy woman stood first, her dark hair and olive skin such at odds with my natural blonde hair and blue eyes. Dahlia had said we were related, but… The woman held out a fine-boned hand for me to shake, and I took it, even though she didn't introduce herself.

She clasped both hands around mine, her dark eyes assessing me with part-joy, part-fear, and a boatload of sadness. One of those hands fell away from mine as she knocked a tear off her cheek.

Blinking back to herself, she cleared her throat. "Sorry, I should have said something before now. My name is Shiloh St. James. I'm your cousin of sorts. We all are." She gestured to the teenager on the couch, her legs tucked underneath her. "That's Poppy." She pointed to the woman in the leather wingback with a book in her hand. "That's Jasper, and you already know Dahlia and Darby. We're your cousins."

That had me taking a step back. "Wait a minute. Darby, you're a St. James, too?"

The Warden shrugged. "About a quarter from my mother's side, which is the only reason I have a boatload of chaos magic running through my veins. All because *somebody* didn't want to hold it anymore," she said, staring at Shiloh like she'd really enjoy lighting her on fire. "Like the grave talker and demigod bullshit wasn't bad enough as is, ass."

Shiloh rolled her eyes, which were turning full black from pupil to sclera as she focused on the Warden. "We've been over this. You needed it at the time, and I don't want it back. Plus, I'm not a witch anymore. Get over it or get rid of it, I don't care which, but stop bringing it up, you little whiner."

Poppy and Dahlia snickered, and Darby flipped Shiloh off.

"I'm the St. James Spell Keeper," Jasper said, eyeing Shiloh and Darby as she unfolded herself from her chair. "I have the knowledge—kind of all of it—from the coven. It's sort of a mess still, but I hold all the secrets for our bloodline. So, yay me."

Poppy, the teenager, waved from her lounge on the couch. "I'm the St. James Oracle, or psychometry which, or psychic... It really depends on who you ask. I kind of, sort of... see the future, but in weird ways. So, super fun. It's actually a huge pain in the ass, but we're making it work."

"Language," Shiloh chided, rolling her eyes that had

somehow turned back to normal. "Nobody likes an Oracle with a dirty mouth."

"You act like you've never met an Oracle a day in your life," Darby muttered. "I haven't met a single one that doesn't cuss like a sailor. And she's a teenager. The *least* you could do is let the girls say ass."

I thought about Malia and had to concur.

"And I'm the mage, I guess, of the St. James Coven," Dahlia offered, tucking her legs under her, her patterned broomstick skirt covering her feet. "Not that there's really a coven of witches anymore, but since I'm more mage than anything else, I guess it doesn't really matter."

"Hey, it does too matter," Poppy said, shooting Dahlia a surly teenager glare hot enough to peel paint. "Just because your power lies more on the mage spectrum doesn't mean that the rest of us—"

"Oh, come on," Shiloh said. "Half of us aren't even witches anymore, but the truth of the matter is, it isn't about being a witch or not. It's about the bloodline and the power it holds. That amulet around your neck is only going to work for so long. It's a Band-Aid. Until you accept the power that your family gave to you, that they sacrificed themselves to make sure you had."

Gratefully, I held on to Theo's hand, his squeeze of reassurance keeping me from falling apart.

"Why does it matter to you whether or not I accept this power? You don't know me."

"I do," Darby said, crossing her legs as she speared me with a knowing look. "You felt like family from the first moment I saw you. I should have known then what that was. I should have helped you find the truth sooner. It wasn't until Sarina told me what was going on did I realize who you were to me. I've lost enough family. I'm not losing you, too. Especially when we all know Josiah isn't just going to let shit lie. He already blew up a bed and breakfast for you and for whatever power is in that ring. If you don't accept it, then he'll steal it right off your finger. And considering he murdered your birth family already, that seems like a big no-no in my book."

"Well, when you put it like that," I muttered, falling onto an open seat. "But the story I've been told doesn't even feel like the truth. There are holes in it and shit missing. How do I know this is the real St. James annulet? How do I know that what he said wasn't one big lie orchestrated by Josiah to get me to do what he wants?"

Theo squeezed my shoulder in support, and I covered it with my hand. "How do I know what's true?"

"I could tell you," Poppy said, holding out her hand. "I could also tell you the truth of what happened to whoever wore that ring before you." She blushed, curling her fingers into a fist. "Only if you want me to, though. It's... up to you."

"If you're concerned about the veracity of it all," Darby offered, "it might be the best way to learn it. Though, Poppy's level of teaching isn't exactly comfortable, you'll learn the truth—probably more than you'd care to know."

I'd had firsthand experience of what Malia could do. I didn't know if I was ready for that level of truth, but it seemed like I didn't have the time to get comfortable with it. Josiah had already blown up a bed and breakfast trying to get to me, had an entire group of women practically on the run because of me. And while I didn't necessarily want to be the martyr of this situation, it was tough not to feel responsible just a little bit, even though it wasn't my burden to carry.

But I needed to know the truth. I had to know if Paul was lying. And I really wanted to know if the bond I shared with Theo was mine to have—if Theo was mine to have.

Gently, I removed the St. James annulet from my finger, passing it over to Poppy.

She patted the cushion next to her, and I reluctantly took it, my gaze finding Theo's as I gathered my courage.

Those gorgeous green eyes glowing with a hint of his wolf hit me, and I knew that even if none of the other things were true, he was still meant for me. He was still mine, and I was still his.

The rest…

"This will be a little uncomfortable, and you might learn things that you didn't want to know," Poppy prefaced before she gently took the hammered gold ring. "I can't promise you'll learn everything you want to, but I'll show you everything there is to see."

With the ring in her palm, she grabbed my hand as if to shake, and then the ghosts of that ring filled my vision, yanking me through time.

I was a child skipping through rain puddles, holding my mama's hand. She twirled me as we danced, the rain soaking into our clothes as we giggled and played, her blonde hair turning brown as it soaked in the rain. The water was almost warm, and the kiss of the breeze danced across my cheeks. I loved her smile, the sparkle of her blue eyes.

"We should head inside, June Bug. It'll be time for dinner soon."

But I didn't want to leave the forest. I could feel my sister just a few short miles to the west, her home so close and so far, all at the same time. Those trees made me think of her. I hung on to the gold ring attached to the necklace that I wore every single day. This ring tied us together, and one day we would be reunited. I just had to be patient.

"*Five more minutes?*" I asked, knowing Mama would give it to me.

"*Five more minutes, June Bug.*"

The scene changed, and then I was at the same house, staring into a mirror.

Mom said that we were identical, but identical witches typically felt each other. They were tied together tighter than any other kind of twin. I wondered if my twin felt Kaden McDonald break my heart when we were fifteen, or that time that I broke my arm when we were ten. I wondered if she had that same scar right above her left eyebrow. I never remembered getting it, it just showed up one day.

Had that been her?

Mom always called her Willow, but I doubted the Jacobs kept that name. Willow and Juniper. Mom always called us her trees. Tall and strong, and made to last. Made to weather the storm.

We were turning eighteen today, and I didn't know if I could hold out not knowing her for much longer. It always felt like a piece of me was missing, a secret little compartment in my heart that always seemed empty.

I twisted the gold ring on my right middle finger, the hammered metal plain for something so special. Mom said it would be hers one day when we were all together again.

I wondered if she missed us like we missed her. If she felt us.

The scene changed again to a birthday party, only it seemed to be half birthday party and half coven meeting.

Staring at my parents, I waited for the ritual to start, the one to call my sister home. I'd been dreaming of this day my whole life, the blessed day of our twenty-first birthday. It had been years—too many years—of wondering if she missed us, of wondering if she wanted to be called home, of praying that when we did, she would know that her real family had always been waiting for her.

I still didn't understand how my parents could possibly have given her up, how they could separate their children like that, how they could allow that monster to take her.

But unfortunately, the reasoning made sense—they'd given up one to save us both, and truth be told, it made sense why Josiah Jacobs would want her: a St. James first born was always formidable, always blessed with immense power. Too bad he didn't have a St. James first born—my sister was younger by about two minutes.

Sitting at the center of the circle, the annulet and my blood would call my twin home. I was ready, ready to end this torment, when the door to our ritual room blew in, exploding into a thousand pieces as the shrapnel flew like daggers into the chamber.

My grandmother had a jagged piece of wood embedded

into her neck, blood pouring down her front as she crumpled to the ground. My mother cradled her in her arms as men stormed into the space, balls of fire hitting my father in the chest as he tried to stand up to them, tried to fight them off.

When the smoke cleared, Josiah Jacobs filed in, his formidable stare, pinning me to the floor. I was in the middle of a casting circle, unable to move from the spot, unable to stop the spell, unable to help my parents, my family. But I had a feeling he knew exactly why we were here today.

"You think you can go back on a deal, and you get to live?" he hissed in my father's face, yanking him from the ground and slamming him into a chair he conjured from nothing. Magical ropes appeared from thin air and tied my father to the spot.

"N-no. W-we—"

Josiah's face was part-sneer, part-malice, and all evil. "You think you can steal what's mine? I felt the start of your spell. You think I'm an idiot?"

His salt-and-pepper hair fell into his eyes, and as he brushed it away, his gaze finally fell on me. "What is this? Fiona, how did you...?"

Realization dawned in his eyes.

"Twins," he breathed. "You had twins, and you gave me the wrong one." He backhanded my mother, knocking her

down. *"You lied to me. Now, my daughter will get all of her twin's power."*

Shaking, I softly told him no, that she wouldn't get anything—not from me. But then he placed his hand on the circle barrier, stealing the magic from it until he could walk right through without so much as a scratch.

"You will give me what I ask for—one way or another. I don't care whose face you wear."

I endured hours of his torture—the burns, the knife wounds, broken bones—but the worst was watching my mother cry as men held her in her chair, peeling her eyelids away so she was forced to look at what he did to me. And then, one by one, life just fell out of them until it was just me. Until it was Josiah and me and all the torture I could possibly withstand.

But what he didn't understand was that with every cut, every burn, every broken bone, I funneled more and more of my magic into the annulet—a ring he could not touch, a ring that could only be unlocked by a St. James witch.

I only had a little bit left, a fraction of my power that I would will away to keep her safe. So when he demanded I give it up, I did. I willed it to her, my twin, my Willow. A sister I would never, ever meet but held in my heart.

But then his eyes traveled down to my bound hand and the gold ring that sat on my middle finger.

Somehow, he knew what it was, what it held. He ripped

it from my skin, the metal burning him so bad that he dropped it.

"What did you do?"

Sucking in ragged breaths, I gave him a bloody smile. "Put it in a spot you can't siphon from, you old bastard. And you can't bargain it, and you can't buy it. You can't steal it. You're shit out of luck, old man."

He let out a rage-filled scream as flames hit my skin, crawling all over me as the pain stole my breath.

And then all that was left was darkness.

I sucked in a breath as if I'd been holding it for decades, tears falling in rivers down my cheeks. Someone cradled me in their arms, but it took forever for me to realize it was Theo, his beautiful voice filtering through the sobs.

"He killed them," I whispered. "He killed all of them. It was just like Paul said. He didn't lie to me. He—"

"It's okay, Cupcake. You're okay."

But I wasn't. I didn't know how anything could be okay ever again. But I would be damned if I didn't accept that power—not after what June had done for me, what she'd sacrificed, the pain she'd endured to give it to me.

"I'll take that ring back now."

Darby crouched in front of me, tears filling her eyes, she took the ring from Poppy's hand and placed it on the center of my palm. "I've been exactly where you are, only the ring had been my father's, not my sister's, and I didn't have to watch him die."

Her gaze fell as did her tears. "I'm sorry for your loss, Fiona. I promise you we'll get him. Fuck the jurisdiction."

My fingers closed over the warm metal, the last remnants of my twin's memory, weighing my soul down like an anchor.

I slipped it onto my finger, allowing my hand to form a fist. Instantly, the power that I had yet to accept filled every inch of me, filled me with new knowledge, a new purpose.

I thought I'd wanted justice before.

Now I just wanted revenge.

CHAPTER 14

FIONA

NEVER IN MY LIFE HAD I WANTED TO CALL IN A favor less.

Unfortunately, I had things to do, and the only way I could do them was call in a boatload of help. That was if "boatload" actually meant a four-and-a-half-foot, sixty-pound ancient vampire with anger issues and a penchant for violence. Calling Ingrid Dubois was near last on my list of enjoyable tasks, especially since the car she'd lent me was in pieces in a backwoods town in Georgia.

Oops.

"I don't know who this is, so state your business," she sang down the line, her childlike voice making the words eerier than they had to be.

"It's Fiona," I said, watching the rest of the St. James witches stare at me like I'd grown another head.

They'd heard my plan, made their positions known, and I'd promptly ignored them. It would be full steam ahead... *if* I could get Ingrid to agree.

"How are you doing, kid? How's tricks?"

I tried to condense the last week into words, the majority of them getting caught in my throat.

"Let's see, I found out that the man I've called 'Father' my whole life is a murdering, torturing prick who has lied to me about just about everything since the dawn of time. And considering I need him to jump on out of hiding so I can cut his fucking head off, I may or may not need your help. Again."

Ingrid seemed to mull that over. "So Josiah Jacobs is not your father?"

And why did that feel good for someone else to say? "Correct."

"By the sheer rage in your tone, I'm guessing the people that actually did give birth to you are really, really dead."

Got it in one. "Also correct."

"And to get your bastard of a kidnapper out in the open, you need to do what, exactly?"

This was the hard part. "I need you to call a council meeting so I can show them exactly how many people he killed when he blew up his coven house. And then once they see the irrefutable evidence that he blew up his own damn house with civilians inside, I need them to put out a warrant for his arrest."

"Because you want him to come after you."

That was the thing about talking to somebody who was over two thousand years old, they knew all the plots already. It was actually kind of nice.

"Maybe, or maybe I—as an ABI agent—want to haul him in myself... Or on the off chance he struggles, lop his fucking head off. Do you think you can call in the meeting tonight?"

"You realize it's past ten already. *Tonight*, tonight?"

I didn't recall stuttering at any point in this conversation, but maybe I needed to make myself clear. "If you'd found out that the man who raised you murdered your whole family—including your twin— would you be so hesitant? Or maybe you need to know that after peeling my mother's eyelids off her face, she was forced to watch her daughter be burned alive? I wonder if you would be as calm as I am right now if this shit had happened to your family."

I felt the silence of the room around me as the other St. James witches stared at me making this phone call. There was even more silence down the line as Ingrid digested what I'd just said.

"No, I'm pretty sure I would have killed at least five

people already. I'll call in an emergency meeting. You need any other help?"

I thought it over. "Can you *not* tell Björn that Darby blew up his car as a precaution to make sure we weren't being followed? I'm already about to be waving a flag in front of a bull. I'd like to live to see the day that fucker takes his last breath."

Ingrid snickered, and I would have given anything to see her face as she tried to hold in the laugh that I knew would burst out of her at any second. "You do realize that she might have to go on the run, right? Björn loves that car."

"It's completely possible, and also not my problem. They can duke it out later. Call me when you know about the meeting."

The call wrapped up shortly after that, and I got to endure the utter silence of the St. James witches.

"No offense," Dahlia said, staring at me like I had just sprouted three more heads, "but you're a little too calm for the level of rage I feel coming off of you. I'm kind of worried you're going to do something stupid."

I looked up at Theo who had seen me just as calm right before I slit someone's throat. He might have been worried, but at no point did he plan on standing in my way. Those glowing green eyes were just as rage-filled as mine likely were, and damn if that didn't make me love him more. Returning my gaze to Dahlia, I figured the truth was about as good as I could do.

"Do you know what my position was in the coven?" I asked to another round of complete silence. "I was his enforcer. Do you think this is the first time I've ever gotten revenge? Do you think this will be the first time I've ever killed someone? I am very capable of having rational thoughts right before I slit someone's throat. Maybe that makes me a psychopath, maybe my give-a-fuck button is broken. Or maybe it just makes me really good at my job. Either way, if you're opposed to my plan, you don't have to participate."

"That's not what I'm saying," Dahlia protested, her hands up in surrender. "I'm just wondering if it's a good idea to waltz into the council, knowing that your former fiancé's family has ties there. We just got you to accept that we're your family. I'd prefer not to lose said family on the first damn day."

The woman did have a point.

"I'm not worried about the Lanes because they always send someone else to do their bidding. I've beat their best already. Unless they want to come at me themselves, I'm not impressed."

Truth be told, I wasn't worried even if they decided to come to me themselves. With the sheer amount of power coursing through my veins, all it would take was a generous snap of my fingers and I would make them hamburger. Maybe I would do worse, considering what Hendrick had planned for me.

"I guess, if you're not worried, but do you really think it's a good idea to go alone?" Jasper pointed out.

"Do you really think it's a good idea for me to show up to a council meeting with every single person I know in tow? I have proof that Josiah killed those people. It's all I need."

"If you say so," Darby said, crossing her arms over her chest, her face telling me she didn't particularly like this plan, but she also wasn't going to stand in my way. "We've already said our piece. We can't make you change your mind."

I was fairly certain that if she could make me change my mind, she would.

I'D GROWN UP IN WHAT MOST WOULD CALL "luxury," but the ivy-coated, turret-having manor that comprised the council was on a whole other level. Darby warned me that getting through security would mean that I would have to lose all my weapons. But I didn't even allow the guard to ask me for them, I simply started slapping potion bombs and athames into the TSA-style bin, polishing it off with my nine-millimeter service weapon.

I was tempted to leave my badge, too, but figured that would have been over the top.

The insanely tall, bald man seemed not quite mage and not quite vampire but a bit of both. I'd never seen a hybrid like that before, but I was amenable to change. Too many of the arcane world hated mixing of the classes. I didn't care so much. What difference did it make if witches and mages decided to fall in love? If vampires wanted something else? If people wanted to be more?

"I heard you borrowed my car," the big man said, and I backed up a step, running into Theo.

"I also heard the Warden blew it up. You'll tell her that she owes me a new one, yes?" he ordered, staring at me like he was daring me to say no.

"Absolutely. You're not mad? It was a very, very pretty car."

He leaned forward. "As many times as she saved my life?" he whispered. "I can't exactly be mad at her. But don't tell her that, deal?"

I crossed my fingers over my heart. "Deal."

"You need to take out all your weapons," Björn instructed Theo, his gaze penetrating as if he were trying to see them through Theo's suit.

"I don't carry weapons," Theo said, his stoic nature making him seem contentious when he was just stating facts. Theo didn't carry weapons—he didn't have to.

Theo *was* a weapon.

Björn took a large sniff. "Shifter?" he asked, putting away a filigreed wand that seemed to have appeared out of nowhere.

Theo inclined his head.

"Fair enough. Follow me. Most of the council is already here."

Since this was an emergency session, it wasn't the ball gowns and tuxes event Darby had warned me about. Still, I followed Björn through the manor, down a grand staircase, and into a rune-filled circle. He conjured a staff from nowhere, banging on the centermost rune three times.

The marble-filled sitting room melted away, and the yank in my gut told me we might not even be on the same plane of existence anymore. The scene in front of me melted away to reveal a wide-open room with ceilings that had to be thirty feet tall. The golden runes embedded in the plaster spoke of protection spell work engrained in the very air itself, each one glowing with heat as they burned bright with magic.

A sea of windows sat behind a raised platform, the night sky full of stars, as the twelve members of the

Arcane Council stared at us. Ingrid's chair matched the rest, her child-sized legs swinging as they failed to reach the floor.

I studied each of the arcaners on the stage. Just as Darby told me she would be, Ingrid was at the outside edge of the group, her sparkly Chucks and hot-pink denim jacket at odds with the suits and classy dresses. Next to her were a trio of women who seemed to hate me on sight, and a pair of men. One of the men sat sideways in his seat, lounging over the armrest, a glass of amber liquid in his fist as he plucked grapes off the bunch in his hand with his teeth. The man next to him stole a grape, shooting a blue ball of magic at Grape Guy when he protested.

There was a large break in the middle, and the next six councilmembers seemed far more austere than the last. There were four men all different in species. One had black eyes, black hair, and skin an odd shade of orange, along with a decent set of horns. Another had blond hair, yellow eyes, and had what appeared to be moss growing on the side of his face. Next to him was a man with blue hair, chugging from a gallon jug of water like he was dying of thirst. The last man had red wind-blown hair tangled around his face as he studied me with intense scrutiny.

The last two arcaners appeared bored to tears. Then

again, if I were an ancient being hauled into a meeting to have someone tattle, I'd be bored as shit, too. The dark-haired male sat leaning to one side, his stubbled chin on his fist. The woman, though, was staring her red-cast eyes right at me.

I knew her—or at least *of* her. Lise Dubois was Magdalena Dubois' maker and an ancient blood mage. Her grandson had caused an all-out war three years back, and the consequences of such had nearly gotten the whole arcane world exposed. How she was still on the council at all was a mystery.

Of all the people in the room, the two I least expected were the Lanes.

But there they were, front and center.

THEO

THE FACT THAT THE LANES WERE ALREADY AT THE council did not give me warm and fuzzy feelings in my gut. I had the distinct impression that at some point we were going to have to fight our way out of here, and I didn't like it one bit.

At Fiona's side, I kept an eye on the council members, on the Lanes, on the giant mage-vampire hybrid that had ties to Ingrid. I didn't quite understand how we would get out of this unscathed, but Fiona had assured me this was the plan that would work.

This was the plan that would keep her breathing and get her father out in the open.

I couldn't possibly begrudge her her revenge. It was Fiona's and mine. It was sixteen years of loss, a lifetime of missed opportunity, it was everything. Josiah Jacobs had taken nearly everything from her—from us—and damn if I was going to stand in my mate's way.

Fiona reached the Lanes, her eyes narrowed as her fingers sparked with magic. She had finally accepted the ring's power, allowing her sister's magic to fill her body and the bond. I felt more tied to her than I ever had before, her golden mating mark shining like a beacon the more she believed in it.

I cradled that small hand in mine, ready to yank her out of there if I so much as sniffed it going sideways.

Björn announced us, the giant of a man bowing low for the council before stating our full names and making me cringe. "Theodoros Philippe Acosta, Second of the Acosta pack, and Special Agent Fiona Willow Acosta-St. James, Arcane Bureau of Investigation."

Fiona snickered, her eyes wide as she tried to keep it together. That was a hell of a lot better than the alternative, but...

Of all the things to make this woman smile, it was my stupid fucking name that did it. And at least her new name didn't make her cry. I'd heard Darby call ahead while the Night Watch's resident revenant made Fiona sit her skinny ass down and eat something. Clementine was absolutely frightening and smelled like pure death, but she made a mean grilled cheese sandwich and tomato soup.

Back when Fiona had been in the Acosta dungeon, grilled cheese and tomato soup had often been the only thing she could keep down. Darby made sure that no one called her a Jacobs again, the name as dead to her as the man who raised her would soon be.

Personally, I loved that in changing Fiona's name, Darby had included my pack to it, adding the extra blanket of safety to my beautiful mate.

"Acosta-St. James?" Amelia scoffed, her lip curled into a sneer. "Don't you mean *Jacobs*? Changing your name doesn't change the fact that you killed my son, most of your coven, and your father, girl. I don't care who they are, no pack can save you from your fate."

Fiona's fingers sparked once again, only this time, Amelia Lane took a smart step back. We both knew Amelia was playing to the crowd. That bitch knew Josiah was alive, Fiona hadn't killed anyone, and if the knuckleheads she'd sent were to be believed, we were giving her exactly what she wanted: Josiah Jacobs out in the open.

If she wanted to kill him, though, she'd have to get in line.

Leveling her gaze at the council, Fiona ignored the two interlopers completely. Stepping forward, she bowed low before addressing them all.

"I realize that my name might cause a stir with you lot

considering its recent change, but I have divorced myself from the Jacobs Coven and that family. I share no blood with Josiah or Belladonna Jacobs," she admitted, her eyes misting over before she swallowed and continued on. "Josiah stole me from my family, he murdered them and tried to take all of the coven's power. Unfortunately for him, it was not his power to take. I can prove that Josiah Jacobs blew up his own damn house and his coven. I just need you to indulge me while I show you exactly what happened."

"And what of our son?" John demanded, stepping forward as if he were ready to touch my mate.

The growl that ripped up my throat had him taking several steps back, abandoning his wife to my proximity while he ran to safety.

"Your son is no concern of mine. I did not agree to be a member of your family or marry your son. Considering what he planned to do to me once he married me—and I mean this with all the disrespect I possibly can—I hope your son is roasting in the pits of Hell with a pitchfork shoved up his ass. Also? Fuck you both."

"As entertaining as all this is, you requested this emergency council meeting, because why, exactly?" the mage next to Lise Dubois asked, his board tone like nails on a chalkboard.

"Josiah Jacobs murdered nearly an entire coven and

several guests—many of whom had friends on this very council," Fiona shot back, her spine straightening as she leveled him with a glare. "And while I don't necessarily give two shits about most of them, the fact that I'm getting blamed for their murders by *certain individuals* makes me mighty keen to plead my case to the highest court we have. If this is too boring for you, my apologies, sir."

And damn if I didn't find that sass of hers so fucking attractive.

"What difference does it make to us whether or not an ABI agent is caught in this tedious crossfire?"

Fiona let out a little growl of her own, and I fought off the urge to bite her again. Fuck, she was magnificent like this. "Maybe if you don't give a shit about your job, you should abandon it and let someone else take over. No offense, but someone as old as you should understand when a power struggle is afoot. The man who raised me wants to steal power. He's ravenous for it, and if he thinks he can get it, he'll kill anyone in his path. It doesn't take a rocket scientist to figure out that maybe you should nip that in the bud before it gets out of hand. Then again, if I have to explain this to you, then maybe you aren't as smart as you think you are."

The man sat up, his black eyes spearing her with

enough hate that I was surprised her hair didn't light on fire.

"And if you can't take criticism," I added, "maybe you shouldn't be in a position of authority. Wasn't it a death mage that nearly exposed all of arcane kind?"

Ingrid snickered, her small hand covering her mouth while the man eating grapes nearly fell out of his chair, laughing.

"He's got you there, Kristof. Maybe you should remove that stick up your ass, yeah?"

The blue-magic-wielding Druid next to Grape Guy leaned forward. "Or maybe just shut up if you don't have anything valuable to say. *Dick.*"

"Come on, child, show us your evidence," Lise Dubois insisted, her red eyes spearing my mate with the level of scrutiny that made me uncomfortable.

Without so much as a whispered word or an herb or an ingredient, Fiona conjured the truth from thin air. Back at the coven house, she'd had to use a considerable level of power, now she was doing it without even so much as a snap of her fingers, showing the council exactly what happened to the Jacobs Coven house while she narrated exactly what was happening.

"We arrived at the Jacobs Coven compound at two thirty in the afternoon on the date of the incident. We were told the event was a birthday party for Belladonna

Jacobs. When the party started at six, we realized that we had been misled and the event was actually an engagement party for me and Hendrick Lane. Josiah Jacobs did not ask me before he promised my hand to Hendrick, and since I was already mated to Theo Acosta, any union promised would be null and void."

"You're lying. Everything that you just said is a complete and utter lie. You knew about the engagement," Amelia screeched, approaching Fiona as if she meant to hit her.

I stepped in between them, my growl letting that bitch know if she moved so much as an inch closer to my mate, she'd turn out just like her son. Dead.

Fiona continued as if Amelia's outburst hadn't even happened. "Naturally, I objected to the engagement publicly and left the ballroom. As you can see here, Hendrick Lane followed and attacked me by slapping my face and attempting to drag me back to the party. To defend myself, I fought back."

Fiona swallowed, continuing the spell as if she were worried that the next part might get us in trouble. "Due to the subterfuge of the situation and the violent response to my objections, we felt the use of unsavory methods to break into the office was necessary as was the deployment of a forbidden object to remove ourselves from the premises. You can see us using the transportation orb. You can see us leaving. Then after we had successfully vacated the premises, Josiah Jacobs entered his own office, procured another transportation orb, and as he was leaving, ignited a blaze among the other forbidden objects inside his safe, detonating his home and endangering the occupants."

The ghostly image of what had transpired in the Jacobs' compound faded away and still, Amelia tried to attack my wife.

Her fingers poised like claws, she tried to get around me to scratch at Fiona, to grab her, to use spells on her, I didn't know which because the crazy bitch was unsuccessful.

"She killed my son. She killed him," she screeched.

"Honestly, Amelia," the dark-haired witch next to Ingrid said, rolling her eyes, "could you please get ahold of yourself? It's obvious the replay spell was not modified, and your son accosted an ABI agent. If she had killed him, it would be just cause."

Now was the time to come clean. Because the truth of it was, Fiona was my mate. She wasn't mated then, but she sure as shit was mated now. Taking Hendrick's life was well within my rights as well—if these people honored pack law.

And that was a big if.

"Fiona didn't kill your son, and neither did Josiah

Jacobs. I ended your bastard of a son's life," I admitted, staring into Amelia's squinty eyes as I confessed to her son's murder. "Pack law states that no mate can be harmed by a rival. Doing so signed his own death warrant. Your son attacked my woman—my mate—in plain view of the public. Did you honestly expect him to live?"

John shoved his wife aside, his face red. "Hendrick wasn't pack, I don't give a shit what you say, your laws don't apply to him."

"No, but *she* is," someone growled from behind us, and I spun to watch my brother, my Alpha, stride into the council chambers. "And our laws apply to her."

Behind him was Wren, followed by Dave LeBlanc and Thomas Gao of the Night Watch. Following them was Darby and Aemon, Shiloh St. James, and Bael, a Prince of Hell, trailed by Magdalena Dubois and Zephyr himself. Darby hadn't just called the council to change Fiona's name.

She'd called in backup, too.

"Fiona Acosta-St. James is a member of the Acosta pack, an honorary member of the LeBlanc pack, an honorary member of the Night Watch, and the Dubois nest. Our laws, our protection apply to her several times over. In no world would touching her *not* earn retribution, and my brother did your son a favor," Nico continued, his glowing gold eyes showing just how close his wolf was to the surface. "Had he lived, he'd be dealing with all of us."

Amelia let out a battle cry, magic sparking from her fingers as she raced toward Fiona. It seemed like everyone moved at once, but only one person reached Amelia Lane before the rest.

Ingrid launched herself from the dais, knocking into the deranged witch faster than a bullet. By the time Ingrid was through, Amelia Lane was in pieces on the floor, and the tiny vamp was stalking toward John like he was Sunday dinner, her little body covered in blood from head to toe.

"You dare come in this house and lie to us? I know all about your assassins in the ABI. I know all about the ones you paid to kidnap an agent. I know all about how they injured a member of my nest. Do you think I'd ever let that stand, John?"

John scrambled back, slipping in his wife's blood and landing hard on his ass. His frantic gaze landed on the bored jackass perched on his seat at the dais. "You're just going to sit there and do nothing? You wouldn't be in that chair if it weren't for me."

"No, I'm not going to do a damn thing. The only reason I'm sitting in this chair is because of *me*. I'm not

Astrid, John. You can't control me, and it looks like your time's about up."

She gave him a little finger wave and blew him a kiss right before Ingrid made mincemeat out of him. He screamed loud and long for a single moment before his voice cut off abruptly, and when Ingrid was done, she licked her fingers clean and daintily wiped at the corners of her mouth.

"Now, we're square," she informed Fiona. "I told you I'd make you take that boon, one way or another."

And damn if the little shit wasn't right.

FIONA

I HAD SEEN A LOT OF BLOODY SHIT IN MY TIME, but watching Ingrid Dubois work, both turned my stomach and had me wanting to bow to her in awe. That's what two thousand years' worth of fighting knowledge got you: a fuck of a lot of skill.

"Considering I thought we were square after the car blew up, I wasn't expecting this. I'm not shitting on it by any means, because I really appreciate not having to look over my shoulder regarding those two for the rest of my life, but... holy shit."

The little monster just shrugged, viscera clinging to one of her ringlets as it moved to and fro. "It was the least I could do. Plus, they were getting on my nerves. It's one thing to lie out in the open, but in these chambers? Not smart."

"Even if it makes us square, I still appreciate everything you did—for calling this meeting, for everything."

I also thoroughly appreciated that I didn't have to lift to finger to take out the Lanes. I had enough to deal with already.

Ingrid flicked goo—which I *did not* want to identify—off the toe of her shoe. "Really, it wasn't that big of a deal. Even though a few of us act like we couldn't be bothered, the Lanes were becoming a problem, and your ex-daddy is nothing to sneeze at, either. Especially since the ABI can't find where he's holing up. The last time the ABI couldn't find somebody, they were hanging out in liminal spaces, which was not fun."

I wasn't sure if I should tell her how versed I was in liminal spaces. I'd had to do the research when trying to get Wren out of fucking Faerie. "I'm not sure that Josiah would use liminal spaces. He doesn't particularly care for the Fae, and I'm pretty sure it's his life goal to never reach the Underworld."

Mostly because he'd fall into the pit and never come out again.

But the whole point of this was to get him out in the open. If the council put out a warrant for his arrest, he'd be hungry for more power—power he would automatically assume he had claim over, power he thought he could use.

"The goal isn't for you to get to him. It's for him to come to me, and then I get to lop his head off, right?"

"I don't know about that." The dark-haired witch stood from her velvet seat, gliding down the dais as she expertly navigated the blood on the marble floor. "Fiona Acosta-St. James, it's a pleasure to meet you. I've been keeping tabs on you since you helped uncover the cadets being stolen from the ABI training camp. I have to say, your career so far has been *eventful*."

The witch's eyes even widened a little bit, telling me she knew a fuck of a lot more than she should.

Aces.

"Solana Pope," she said, outstretching her hand for me to shake. Reluctantly I took it, and the woman covered my hand with hers. "My cousin was one of the women taken. I hear your pack has people looking for her. When she is returned to her family, I will be calling on the Acosta pack to give my thanks. Until then, you will have my advice."

Her grip got tighter, making a growl rip up Theo's throat. She sliced a glare at my mate. "Hush. I'm giving her a gift." She returned her gaze to me. "You must be the coven leader for your whole family line. The St. James

Coven has been without a qualified leader for far too long. It is imperative that you accept the mantle."

I yanked my hand from hers, backing up a step. "I didn't even know I was a St. James before this week. And even though I'm no spring chicken, I'm still one of the younger members. Why can't one of the others take the lead?"

Solana gave me a patient smile while she ticked off the known members on her fingers. "The youngest, Poppy, for obvious reasons. Jasper is the Spell Keeper—she already has a purpose. Shiloh isn't a witch anymore, her demon mate made sure of that. Magically, Dahlia is mostly mage and is too different to even qualify as a witch. All that leaves is Darby, and I must say the Warden is busy enough. You're the only one to take it, the only one the council trusts to take it, anyway."

But if I took the coven leader position, then I would have to hand in my badge. The conflict of interest would be too great. Then again, being a member of the Acosta pack, an honorary LeBlanc pack member, and all the rest, meant my conflicts of interest we're getting a little too numerous to keep that badge, anyway.

"What if I say no?" I asked, just to get all my ducks in a row. "What if I say I don't want to belong to a coven ever again? Considering how the last one kind of exploded, being a member doesn't seem like a good idea."

"And what if I told you, you didn't have a choice? Think of it this way, you'll do a hell of a lot more good as a coven leader than you ever would with that badge. The writing is on the wall, Fiona. The corruption of the ABI is bigger than we ever thought. Plus, coven leaders have a decent amount of leeway, a decent amount of influence. Even though it seems you have that in spades, one of these days you're going to need it. Trust me."

"Ultimatums rarely work on me," I warned, knowing I was probably taking this a step too far.

"It's a good thing I'm not giving you an ultimatum. I'm giving you an order. Fiona Acosta-St. James, you are now the leader of the St. James Coven. You will be required to police your members accordingly. Don't worry. You'll benefit from the title sooner rather than later."

"Speaking of titles," the lax shifter with the grapes said, following Solana down the dais. "Björn introduced you as the Acosta Second." His gaze flicked from Theo to Nico. "He's not your Second. He's your Omega. Trying to pigeonhole him into Second position is hurting him."

"And you are who, exactly?" Theo asked, shifting so he was in between his brother and the shifter.

"The name is Kato. Trust me when I say I know pack positions rather well—especially since I'm the Omega Supreme for North America. I'm not sure when you lot decided Omegas were the outcasts, but I can assure you, we're not. There's a reason the saying goes 'Alpha *and* Omega.' We go together."

"What's the difference between a Second and an Omega?" Nico asked, standing in front of his big brother like they were leapfrogging to protect each other.

"A Second follows the Alpha's orders. An Omega keeps the Alpha in check. It is a balance, a way to keep the ship running at all times. A way to properly protect your pack. The Alpha is in front, the Omega is behind, making sure there's no stragglers, no weak spots. If the Alpha is the head, the Omega is the neck. It's an honor. Omegas can typically sense relationships and emotional ties—they can understand the health of their pack at just a glance."

Kato focused on Theo. "You can see how big your mate's bonds are, how tight. So can I. You've always been an Omega. Embrace it. It'll serve you well."

Nico stared at his brother with a fresh set of eyes. "It's not like you aren't already doing the job. The last three years, you've kept my ass out of the fire more times than I can count."

Theo frowned, staring at his feet. "You needed the help, and your mate was gone. What was I supposed to do? Let the pack fall apart? It's not a big deal."

Nico stared at the ceiling like he was praying for

patience. "I'm going to pretend you didn't say that, and that you don't sound exactly like your wife when you downplay all the good things you've done. It's annoying. Quit it."

I pursed my lips, trying not to snicker. Nico wasn't wrong.

"When Wyatt gets back, I will make him my Second. Until then, Theo, you are the Acosta Omega. Thank you for all you have done for us."

Theo waved his brother off. "Yeah, yeah. I'm awesome. Whatever."

But the recognition was something he needed. My mate needed to know he was appreciated, that his pack loved him, that it wasn't just following orders day after day, year after year. He had more than that—he deserved more than that.

"Well, now that's done," Kato said, brushing off his hands, "I'm going to go do something completely debased to get the taste of responsibility out of my mouth. Have fun."

And with little more than a finger wave, Kato sauntered off, giving the blue-magic-wielding Druid a noogie as he exited the council chambers.

"You will have to turn in that badge sooner rather than later," Solana murmured, her gaze piercing. "Trust me, it'll all work out in the end."

But a part of me didn't believe her one bit.

THE ABI HEADQUARTERS IN KNOXVILLE WAS A place I tried to avoid at all costs. It was bad enough that the Savannah building made my skin crawl, but the Knoxville one had rather recently been completely invaded, with too many agents losing their lives in a matter of minutes to a horde of unnested vamps.

I wasn't a fan of the place, and I was even less of a fan of what I was about to do.

Theo and I had managed to give out hugs and thanks to all the awesome people who had shown up to support us at the council meeting, and after a decent amount of thought—and Darby pestering me until I almost lost my mind—I decided Solana wasn't exactly wrong.

In my short tenure as an agent, not only had I been kidnapped by an instructor before I even made it out of boot camp, but I'd realized that the ABI was no better than the rest of the arcane community.

There were no good guys and bad guys.

There was just a bunch of people trying to survive.

I didn't have influence here. I didn't have a way to make things better. And unfortunately, I had learned that this place was just as corrupt as any other.

As a coven leader—even as small a coven as the St.

James one was—I could make a difference. More of a difference than I ever could as an agent.

At the front desk, I checked in for our meeting with Director Sarina Kenzari. I'd met the director years ago during the Battle of Knoxville, and she had not-so-smartly stolen a transportation orb from me. Her going all cowboy on the situation had nearly gotten her killed, but considering she hadn't gotten me in trouble for the orb, I decided to keep my mouth shut on that front.

"I have an appointment," I told the receptionist before taking a seat and settling in for a long wait.

Resting my head on Theo's shoulder, I wondered how long it would take for my—*not*—father to finally come out of hiding. How long would I be waiting for him? That was the funny thing about revenge. Most people were vastly impatient and wished to dole out their wrath as soon as possible.

Not me.

I wanted it to take a long time. I wanted him to wonder if I was around every corner, about to strike at any second. Maybe that made me a bad person, but considering the torture he'd put my twin through, Josiah Jacobs deserved a little psychological warfare.

"About time you showed up," Sarina said, the Oracle practically sneaking up on us.

Maybe it was the sleep deprivation, maybe it was the

lack of food, but I just wasn't in the mood for Oracle games.

"Can you still read my mind, or does this handy dandy little necklace prevent that, too?" I asked, staring into her whiskey-colored eyes as I tried to assess just how much trouble she was going to give me.

She shot me a censuring glare. "Come on, let's go into a conference room."

Reluctantly, Theo and I got up, and we followed the director through the bustling lobby.

She led us into a darkened room, the table made to look like real wood but any arcaner would know it wasn't. The chairs were plastic, and it was just like any other human office building: cheap furniture, cheap construction, and without a lick of personality.

"I have about ten meetings after this, so we're going to get right to it. First, I don't exactly advertise that I can read people's minds, so the next time you walk through here, maybe don't announce that to the world at large? Second, yes, I will accept your badge and your service weapon, and I will make sure your exemplary service record is put in your file should you ever want to come back. Third, when Darby told you to get your act together, she did not mean be an ABI agent. I'm very glad you haven't veered too far off Fate's path, though. It's good to see the ship righting itself."

I fought off the urge to growl. "Any other sage advice you want to give me?"

"When it comes down to it? Remember who your enemies are."

With that cryptic statement, Sarina gave us a hug, collected my badge and gun, and exited the room as if she hadn't been completely vague as fuck.

Slowly, we shuffled out to the lobby, ready to put this to bed. Honestly, I would just really enjoy not sleeping in a car or being interrupted while I made out with my husband. *Husband.* I snickered, holding onto Theo's hand, enjoying how small mine was in his.

We were almost home free when a large man barreled into my shoulder, nearly knocking me on my ass. He latched onto my arm, but no matter the growl that came from Theo's throat or my magic shoving him away, he wouldn't let me go. His eyes were unfocused, his pupils blown, as the sickly scent of almonds wafted from his skin.

I knew that scent very well. I'd grown up with it.

Cyanide.

But more, it was cyanide mixed with a compulsion spell. The man's grip tightened as he shoved a folded piece of paper into my hand. His mouth foamed as the convulsions started, but only when I took the paper from him did he let me go, collapsing onto the floor before eventually, his entire body stopped moving altogether.

"What the fuck was that?" Theo growled, hooking me by the waist and pulling me away from the now-very-dead messenger in the ABI lobby as agents scrambled around like ants.

Reluctantly, I opened the paper, the loopy scroll of my mother's handwriting making my stomach drop. But Belladonna Jacobs was not my mother, she never had been. And she had most definitely known what her husband had done to my real family.

To my real mother.

To my twin.

> *I HAVE SOMETHING YOU WANT. THAT IS, UNLESS YOU EXPECT ALL THE MEN IN YOUR LIFE TO DIE FOR YOU. I'LL TELL PAUL YOU SAID HI EITHER WAY. MY GARDEN IS CALLING MY NAME.*
> *—MOTHER*

That dirty fucking bitch.

Belladonna Jacobs was a master of exactly one thing: poisons. Taking her name just a little too literally, she had helped my father keep his power when even sweetening magic hadn't done the trick. That bitch still had spies on her payroll.

Spies in the ABI.

Spies who knew just where to deliver her missive.

And now she had Paul, a man who had only ever looked out for me, who'd only ever helped me.

She wanted a war?

I'd fucking bring her one.

CHAPTER 17

FIONA

The benefits of being the St. James Coven leader included access to a boatload of magic. Magic that I fully intended to use to burn my mother to the ground. But first, I had to stop calling her my mother.

Belladonna Jacobs was not my mother, had never been. She never carried me in her womb, never pushed me out of her body. She hadn't so much as kissed a single boo-boo or tended to a single fever. She hadn't done a single thing to be given that honor. Not. Fucking. One.

I had been raised by nannies, not the kind gentle soul that June had her whole life.

I would have killed to have the mother June had. I would have sold my soul for it. Instead, I had the cold, calculating beast who had every intention of selling me off for more power.

Who thought it was a good idea for parents to be able to just bargain children away?

Who thought it was right to make someone's life no more than currency?

Instead of going through the ABI front doors, I latched on to Theo's hand and turned down a hallway, our presence basically ignored due to the commotion. I needed to make a portal, and I was no longer worried about whether or not I'd open a gate to Hell or Faerie or Timbuktu. I needed to get somewhere, and in a hurry, and this time a fast car just wouldn't do.

I stopped dead in the corridor when Sarina rounded the corner, the Oracle passing over my badge and gun and silently guiding us to a storage room with all the witchy ingredients I could possibly need.

"I'll take the badge and gun back after you're done killing your kidnappers. Try not to make a mess of things," she said, before ducking right back out of the door to attend to the dead man in her lobby.

"How the fuck does she know all that? How did she know we were coming? And what the fuck did that note say?"

Theo's questions made my eye twitch, but I passed over the parchment as I dug through spell ingredients, looking for a box of chalk. Before I accepted June's power, it would have taken at least twenty ingredients and a bowl of chicken blood to get a portal open. Now, all I needed was to create a door on a wall and a snap of my fingers.

Don't get me wrong, I'd need more than that if I was going to face down Belladonna, but it was a fucking start.

Theo's concerned gaze fell on me. I couldn't see it, but I felt it. "You don't expect us to just waltz in there without a plan, do you?" Theo asked, and I considered it a very stupid question.

"I have a plan," I said simply. "I'm going to meet her just like she asked me to, and then I'm going to cut her fucking head off. There. That's the plan. Ready?"

"Cupcake," he said softly, but I really couldn't be swayed by a soft tone of voice with a gentle hand on my shoulder and a kiss to my cheek.

I'd turned off the emotional part of my brain. There were no emotions. There wasn't a single care in the world. All I needed to do was handle business. I'd worry about emotions later.

"Do you honestly want me to believe that you can take her life just like that? She raised you, Fiona. She—"

My hand finally closed around the chalk, and I realized I was just about done with being patronized for the rest of forever.

"See, that's the difference between you and me. You actually had a mother. Belladonna Jacobs let nannies raise me, and now, I find out that she didn't even carry me. She fucking stole another woman's child and tried to raise her as her own. Only, she doesn't have a maternal bone in her body, so somebody else had to do it. Somebody else had to teach me right from wrong. Someone else had to teach me spells. Someone else had to make me a functioning adult with a mind of my own and a scant number of scruples. It sure as shit wasn't her."

I snatched a few more ingredients in the middle of my tirade, beginning the process for antidotes since her favorite method of murder was poison.

"And now she has my oldest friend in the world hostage, and she's probably going to try to poison him to death right in front of me because she's just that much of a bitch. So, my plan is to whip up a shit-ton of antidotes, take all the ammo that I can find and maybe a knife or two, and hunt her ass down. And then I'm going to make sure she dies slow and painful, knowing she'll never beat me. Knowing that I fucking won, that I found my family, that I found my happiness, and then for however many seconds she has left, she'll know for certain that I never gave her what she wanted."

And my voice might have gotten louder and louder with every word I said. Also, the glass canisters filled with potions and ingredients might have been floating in the air. And the ground may or may not have been shaking just a little bit. And if my fingers were full-on lightning bolts of magic, well, I couldn't really help that.

"Do you honestly believe that she wasn't in the passenger seat right next to him, driving this train? That she didn't know who she was killing? That she didn't know what her husband had done? No, she knew. She knew that she wasn't my mother, that I was stolen, and she didn't lift a fucking finger to change that fact. So, no, I don't give a shit about that woman, and I will gladly spill her blood the first fucking chance I get."

Okay, so the emotional part of my brain wasn't exactly fully toggled in the "Off" position. Still, I was going to get shit done.

One look at Theo's face, though, had my rage spiking just a little. Because what was that fucker doing?

Grinning like a damn loon, that's what.

"Why are you smiling at me like that?"

He rubbed at the stubble on his cheek, his smile not slipping a millimeter. "Because you're fucking gorgeous like this, all full of wrath, taking care of the people you love. You might be batshit crazy right now, but you're *my* batshit crazy."

He hooked me around the middle, drawing me in as he completely ignored the control I *did not* have over this new power boost.

"Just to clarify the plan here—are we doing murder now or not? I just need to know what's on the table, because a few days ago, you said we weren't killing anyone. I'm ready for whatever, but—"

My eye may or may not have actually twitched. "That was when we were on the run, and I didn't want a trail of bodies leading right to us. We're not on the run anymore. You want to know if murder is on the table again? How about this, you go ahead and get yourself a knife and a fork because I fully intend on ending her life and anyone else she might have in her pocket that stands in my way."

Theo's smile—amazingly enough—went wider, and if I didn't have shit to do, I would have jumped his bones on the spot. "Whatever you need, Cupcake. I'll always have your back."

I sucked in a trembling breath. That's when reality truly set in: Theo would follow me to the ends of the earth. He would back me up in battle. He would fight by my side through whatever.

He would always be my family.

No matter what.

"I love you. You know that, right?" I whispered, knowing this wasn't the best time to get all mushy but needing it said all the same.

His smile slipped as he brought his lips to mine, the

searing heat of his kiss telling me that he more than knew my heart. "You know I love you, too. Right?"

"Yeah," I said on a sigh. "Now let's get this shit done."

THE FAMILIAR FOREST SURROUNDING THE JACOBS property was astonishingly loud as we slipped through the portal from the ABI, the birds and animals doing the work of disguising our movements. I couldn't tell if it was a welcome or a warning, but I was just glad that we didn't have to be silent. Navigating through any forest was always loud as shit. It didn't matter if you were walking on two feet or four.

Theo kept his eyes peeled for traps as I set my feelers out for something lying in wait, a snare that Belladonna had sprung. Uncertainty filled my gut when I didn't find anything, no tripwires, no magical bombs, no potions... Just a whole load of fuck all. Using this brand-new power, I shoved it outward, trying to find something, anything that told me what Belladonna had in store for us.

She wasn't exactly a slouch in the planning department, so there had to be more. Right?

Or maybe she wasn't prepared. She might have spies in the ABI, but she didn't know how fast we could move now. It was possible she didn't expect me to come this fast, to act without impunity for my oldest friend in the world.

Then again, Belladonna was a textbook narcissist, so maybe she didn't quite understand what someone would do for a person they cared about.

Pulling on a cloak of obfuscation magic, I followed Theo as he led me through the trees, knowing that at no point would she ever expect my mate to come with me.

She didn't think highly of shifters. Hell, she didn't think highly of most other arcane classes, assuming witches were the superior ones. But that's where she really failed, because she had no idea what they were capable of.

What Theo was capable of.

Theo jumped into his wolf form, the pale-white fur practically shining like a beacon in the night. Those brilliant green eyes glowed like fireflies as he gave me a slight nod before taking off into the forest, scenting out whatever traps my magic might have missed.

She wasn't going to get away with this, no way, no how.

A few minutes later, Theo appeared between the trees, a beckoning *yip* propelling me forward. I followed him through the trees to a spot I had only seen as a child. Belladonna's garden was not like mine or the coven's down the hill. Hers was full of every single poisonous plant there was. Set in a grove of Hemlock trees, the fence was lined in Oleander and Azaleas. Foxglove, Lily of the Valley, and Jimson Weed filled the garden, along with ornamental peach trees and Deadly Nightshade and of course, Belladonna.

It made sense that she was waiting for us, but it wasn't just Paul with her. My large friend lay listless, hugging a small body to his chest. Tears streamed down his face as he brushed the hair out of a little girl's eyes. It didn't matter that the girl wasn't breathing, wasn't moving, her wide-open stare telling me that she had most certainly taken her last breath.

I knew that little girl.

It was Cora, Paul's niece, and she had just turned five not six months ago.

Covering my mouth, I choked down a sob as I watched a woman I had once called "Mother" skip around a pile of bodies. Cora was just the smallest, but there were others—so many others. Paul had been worried about his family, worried that telling me my origins could end up hurting them. I had a feeling he'd always expected Josiah to do the killing.

Oh, how stupid we had been.

She killed them all, and for what?

To prove that she was a monster just like Josiah?

To prove that I should take her seriously?

Or maybe it was just because she wanted to.

I swallowed, tears filling my eyes as I tried not to lose it. "They're all—"

Theo grabbed my hand, his fingers squeezing mine as he nodded. "Dead, Cupcake. All but him, but..."

The scent of bitter almonds filtered through the air, luckily lacking the compulsion magic her messenger had. But I knew by the sluggish way Paul was moving, he'd already been poisoned. There wasn't much time left if I wanted to save him, and even if there were, I wasn't sure he'd want me to.

Still, she would have my revenge. Maybe Paul's, too.

But we had to play this smart. Sure, Belladonna might be a sadistic, unhinged bitch, but if she had managed to poison an entire family at once, she was smarter than I'd given her credit for.

"I know you're out there," she sang, skipping around the pile of bodies like she was having the time of her life. "Come out, come out, wherever you are."

This was not the mother who'd raised me—and yes, I used that term loosely. This wasn't the perfectly poised debutant who wouldn't get out of bed without makeup on. I didn't recognize this woman, and I sure as shit didn't want to.

I didn't have a complete handle on the brand-new powers that I now possessed, but I did know what I was capable of. I had enough hate coursing through my veins that when I thought about a bolt of lightning hitting six inches away from her foot, it simply just happened.

The force of the blast knocked her away from the deceased she was desecrating, her body flying through the air like a rag doll. She landed several feet away, her mouth full of dirt, her limbs at odd angles. Slowly, she struggled to stand, the electricity likely still frying her brain cells.

"What? You don't like how I play, *Mother*? Are you sure you don't want to see the rest of my new tricks?" I called, knowing she would never pinpoint my location.

But I wanted her to see my face when she took her last breath, wanted her to know it was me who took her down. I took a step out from the tree line, shedding my obfuscation magic so she could see just who was putting her in her place.

She scrambled to her feet, her left shoe long gone. Lopsided, she limped to Paul, a ball of magic forming in her palm. But as powerful as she was, I knew I had more than her.

"You think I won't kill him, too?" she screeched, a crazed look in her eyes that hadn't been there before.

"Do you honestly believe that I don't know he's dead already? *Mother*."

Her arm twitched as she rolled her head on her neck. "Stop calling me that."

"What? Mother?" I asked, stalking forward. "What? You don't like that name? Is it because I know who you really are? A thieving, murdering, sadistic bitch."

"I didn't kill them. Your father did that."

"He's not my fucking father, and you aren't my mother. And if you honestly want me to believe that you weren't part of it, maybe you shouldn't have stayed with him my whole life, giving in to his every fucking whim. I know all about the bodies you buried, and I know they're fertilizer for your fucking plants."

Her crazed eyes widened. "You have to give it to me. You have to give it to me before he takes it."

"Give you what? The St. James annulet? If you want it, you're going to have to come and fucking get it."

"I'll kill him. I'll shove his body so full of poisons, you'll watch him liquefy right in front of you." Somehow, some way, she reached down and pulled Paul from the ground, his big body leaning against her as she struggled to hold him up. "You think I won't do it? I will. Hand over that fucking ring."

Did she not understand that the ring was merely a placeholder? There was nothing in it now. It was simply a golden band. The power didn't reside in the ring, it lived in me.

Paul listlessly met my gaze, the effect of the poison racing through his veins as he struggled to breathe. There wasn't a damn thing I could do for him except allow him his revenge.

Closing my eyes, I conjured the image of a dagger, a perfect one just for him. Just like Zephyr told me to, I saw it in my mind, placing it right in his hand, closing his feeble fingers around the hilt. When I opened them again, that perfect dagger was in his fist.

I didn't believe he had it in him, the poison too much for anyone to withstand, but he whipped around and drove that dagger right into Belladonna's heart. Shock suffused her expression as she stumbled backward, her hands pathetically attempting to grasp the blade in her chest.

She tripped over her own feet, landing right next to the pile of bodies she had just been dancing around, the blade protruding from her chest as she moaned out a plea for help. Paul collapsed to his hands and knees, and oh, so slowly, he crawled toward her. Gripping that blade, he ripped it down, tearing through her heart like she had done him.

That was just about all the strength Paul had. He collapsed right next to her, his breaths coming in labored pants.

Theo and I raced across the grass as I pulled one of

the many antidotes from my pocket. I plucked the stopper from the vial, trying to get the antidote into his mouth.

"Don't bother," he murmured, just those two words almost too much. "It's too late, anyway."

"It's not," I insisted, but I knew the truth.

If I were in Paul's shoes, and all my family was dead around me, I didn't think I'd want the antidote, either.

"You still have time."

His gaze slowly fell on his niece and then his sisters, his mother, his brother-in-law. "And where is their time? I spent my whole life protecting them, and I failed. The jig is up, my friend. It's time to hang up my hat."

Tears hit my eyes as I struggled to swallow. Years of friendship, of love, and I could barely say a word. I'd known him my whole life. He was my brother, not by blood, but by deed. Letting him go was killing me.

"How am I supposed to let you go?" I asked, clutching his hand. I'd been so mad at him, so betrayed, but in the end, it hadn't been his fault.

"Easy as breathing, Fi. But stay with me?"

Paul had always stayed with me, backed me up. "Always."

He chuckled a little, blood coming to his lips when he started to cough. "Glad you found someone to deal with your ass. F-feel better about l-leaving you behind. Don't give him t-too m-much t-trouble."

"I won't," I lied, and we both knew it. I was a pain in the ass. Luckily, Theo loved it.

Paul smiled, his mouth pulling into a bloody grin. "Li—"

But he never finished the word, his life leaving him in a moment. One second, he was there, and the next, he was gone. I fought off the urge to scream, the pain tearing at my heart almost too much.

A gentle hand squeezed my shoulder, but it wasn't Theo. Startled, I jumped to my feet, only to find a beautiful white-haired woman standing behind me with a scythe in her hand. Theo tucked me behind him, and backed away, but the woman only smiled, her black wings shivering just a bit.

"I'm not here for you. I'm here for them," she said, tipping her chin at the bodies.

Only, they weren't bodies anymore. Paul and Cora stood holding hands, the rest of his family falling behind him, all of them looking at the woman who could only be Death. Their forms were semi-transparent and completely silent, but it was a comfort to see them all the same. It was almost as if he wasn't quite gone, just on vacation somewhere, ready to return at any minute.

"Sloane? Darby's sister?" I asked, peeking around Theo's big body.

She smiled, inclining her head. "And you're Fiona and Theo. I've met your sister. She told me to tell you hello."

As kind as that was, it just made my heart hurt more. Feeling her death had been horrifying, but somehow this managed to hurt worse. Still, a deity essentially passed me a note from the beyond.

I swallowed down my pain and gave her a tremulous smile. "Thank you. If you don't mind saying hey back if you get a chance..."

"Of course." Her gaze went from me to Paul and back. "They'll be fine, you know? It's nice where they're going."

And as much as it helped, my heart was still breaking.

Sloane held out a hand for Cora, the two of them striking up a conversation I couldn't hear, and before I knew it, the whole family disappeared, their bodies melting away in the night.

All that was left was the husk of my heart and the truth that the worst was yet to come.

THEO

IF I COULD GO THE REST OF MY LIFE WITHOUT clutching a sobbing mate to my chest while she mourned another wrong done to her, that would just be fantastic. Instead, I was holding the most beautiful woman in my arms, and she was crying hysterical tears once again because we'd just watched her oldest friend lose his life against...

I kept wanting to call Belladonna Jacobs Fiona's mother, but whatever that woman was, she didn't have a single mothering bone in her entire body.

No mother would kill so indiscriminately, so callously.

No mother would do what she had done.

My ass in the dirt, I sifted my fingers through Fiona's pinky-purple hair, hoping that I was strong enough to help her through this one. No, the job wasn't done, but for this one moment, she needed to grieve. She needed to mourn. She needed to feel. She had tried so hard to get there in time, but I had known as soon as that note hit her hand that the deck had been stacked against us.

Because if there was one thing I knew about the awful people that raised her, it was that they would do whatever it took to get what they wanted.

Especially if it meant hurting Fiona.

Considering I was rather put out that it would likely be bad form to kick a corpse, all I could do was help her through it. All I could do was hang on—and let her feel. Her misery filled our bond, the loss of her friend, the loss of his family almost too much for her to bear.

And even though we were assured by the Angel of Death herself that Paul's family would be going to a better place, it didn't take the sting out of the wound one bit. Personally, I thought Belladonna got off too easy. Then again, I wasn't sure how to torture someone who didn't have a heart.

Would pain have done it? Or would I have had to call in the big guns and ask one of our witchy friends to strip that bitch of all her power like Wren had done to her family? Was this what happened when you lived too long? You got too bold, too complacent, too hungry for power with nothing to satisfy you other than the pain of others.

"W-why?" Fiona asked, but I had a feeling she didn't expect me to answer the question. "Why would she do this? What goal does it serve to kill his whole family? To murder them all?"

There was no good answer.

There was no good reason.

There was nothing—no comfort, no revenge, no nothing.

"And Sloane just took the body so I can't even set her shitty corpse on fire."

It was not appropriate for me to laugh at this particular juncture, but I did. I laughed long and hard, holding my mate to my chest as the poison of it all started flooding out of her. Belladonna had been nothing but poison—a toxic creature with no real purpose other than to kill.

Eventually Fiona started laughing alongside me, burying her face in my shoulder as her whole body shook with inappropriate mirth. But it was just us, and my mate could laugh, she could cry, she could scream—anything she needed.

We likely would have continued on laughing forever if I hadn't felt the prick of eyes on us.

Someone was out there.

Someone was watching.

And they didn't feel friendly.

I clutched Fiona tighter to me, moving my lips to her ear.

"Someone's in the forest," I murmured, hoping it wasn't another shifter that could hear the quickening of our heartbeats or my whispered words.

Fiona gave me the most imperceptible of nods, letting me know she completely understood the situation. It wasn't fair. She needed more time—we needed more time.

"Do you have a bead on how many?" she whispered, her mouth barely moving against my skin as she tucked her arms around her body. Her hands slowly moved for the potions on her belt and the gun in the holster.

Doing my best to be subtle, I indicated "no," but I had a feeling it was not a small number by any stretch of the imagination. No, I had a feeling we were surrounded. I allowed my wolf to drive for a second, taking the scents of the forest, the sounds. It had to be about twenty at least.

Twenty arcaners. All moving toward us at once.

"How do you want to play it, Cupcake? Calm, cool, and collected, or your specialty?" Was I being an asshole? Absolutely. But getting a rise out of her was more important than feelings right then.

"My specialty?" she growled, pulling away as her exquisite blue eyes sparked with both power and ire.

I couldn't help the sly smile that formed on my lips, especially as a gorgeous flush hit her chest. Granted, that flush was due to the fact she was trying not to murder me, and not an impending orgasm, but I'd take it all the same.

I quirked an eyebrow. "Full steam ahead, guns blazing, worry about the consequences later. Your specialty, Cupcake."

Sparks of lightning arced off her fingers as those blue eyes began to glow.

"Are you trying to piss me off?" she asked, tilting her head to the side.

Smiling wide now, I gave her a nod, helping her to her feet. "Mad is better than sad right now, right?"

Realization dawned on her face, the reality of the situation hitting her square in the chest. We were surrounded. We were in danger. The people out in that forest weren't there for shits and giggles. They were there to kill us. Josiah Jacobs was making his stand, and we were about to be cannon fodder.

Yeah, I wanted her mad. I wanted her furious. I wanted her to use that rage, that fire, and make it out of this. I wanted her to live.

"You want to see mad?" she asked, backing away from me as a sly smile tipped up her lips.

"Fuck, yeah, I want to see mad. Give them hell, Cupcake."

Tears filled her eyes. Yeah, this was bad. We were surrounded, on our own, and had no idea who we were up against. And none of it—Paul's death, losing him, losing her family—was fair. We hadn't had enough time. Not enough happiness. Not enough laughter. There was never enough—there never would be with her.

"Love you," she mouthed as arcs of lightning flew from her body. Slamming into the ground, their bolts spread through the trees to hit our enemies.

I jumped to my wolf, giving him free rein, but it didn't take my animal to sniff out the arcaners that had come for us. No, they came all on their own, racing toward my mate as if she had set off a starter pistol.

Balls of magic flew through the air toward us as Fiona's power ramped up. The St. James annulet had given her more power than she could use, the reaches of it still unknown to us. But she would use it all if she had to. Fiona wasn't going to lose another person in her life, not without putting up a fight.

A vampire raced for her as a sorcerer slammed his staff into the ground, the earth reaching up and knocking us all off our feet. All except my mate, who directed her power at the asshole responsible. Arcs of lightning, of pure, unadulterated magic tore through the ground, chewing through it as if it were hunting for prey. And it found exactly what it was looking for. Blue bolts of energy reached the sorcerer, burning him to a crisp.

That left a vampire for me, and I leapt through the air, colliding with him before he could tear his claws into her. My teeth found his throat before his talons could find me. A single shake of my head, and the vampire was a withered husk, his body desiccating faster than I could blink. All that was left of him were his clothes and a golden shield with a very specific logo on it.

Two interlocking crescent moons and an all-seeing eye.

I just killed an ABI agent—a dirty one.

It didn't make sense why these people would be after us. Why would they attack an agent, one of their own? There was no warrant out for Fiona's arrest, no call to attack her.

Unless...

Sarina had handed over Fiona's badge and gun because she knew. That fucking Oracle knew exactly what would happen, exactly what she would need.

Let's just hope when she was working out her vague as fuck plans, she scheduled in a call for backup while she was at it.

I had a feeling we would need it.

A witch tossed an acid bomb at Fiona's feet, the toxic chemical splashing up on her shoes and eating away at her jeans. I set my sights on her next, allowing Fiona to cut through a warlock whose power was far inferior to hers.

My fangs ripped into the witch's shoulder, into the very arm that tossed the acid at my mate. One twitch of my jaw later, and that arm was on the ground, and that witch was screaming her agonized cries into the night.

I stopped waiting for them to attack, stopped waiting for Fiona to choose her targets, and went about systematically demolishing them one by fucking one. Every single one of them was a threat, and if they were there to hurt my wife, well, then, they were nothing more than fucking kibble, now, weren't they?

A Druid worked his magic, filling the clearing with a whipping wind, carrying blazing fire. I went for him next, but Fiona seemed to pluck the fire from the very air, sending it back to him. The ball of flames hit him square in the chest, knocking him off his feet and into the trees. That wind didn't subside, and as the earth began to rock and roll, I had a feeling he might have been down, but he wasn't out.

I fought off the urge to follow him into the trees, the scent of a trap too strong for me to ignore. Instead, I chose to return to Fiona. I was mere feet away when something large slammed into me from the side, knocking my wolf off all four feet as I landed in the dirt.

A growl rumbled in a giant chest, the ghoul practically salivating as it waited for me to attack. I wasn't a huge fan of ghouls. Other than Hannah, my experience with them had been minimal at best, the whole flesh-eating business making them not exactly welcome in Savannah.

Most undead things weren't welcome in Savannah.

What I did know of ghouls equated to knowing that they were strong, fast, and fucking hard to kill.

The giant reached for me, moving far faster than I would have liked him to. His large hands tried to grip my fur as his wide-open maw snapped its teeth together, the *clack* sending shivers down my spine.

Getting eaten was at the very bottom of the list of happy things.

He lunged, trying to latch onto me, but I raced around him, managing to get his back. My teeth found the tender skin of his neck, and I shook my head, hoping to decapitate the big bastard. But I'd been too slow. The ghoul yanked me from his back, tossing me away from him.

The ground and I met again, this time harder, and I felt something pop. With nothing for it, I leapt back to two feet, snapping my shoulder back into socket as I reached for the knife in my belt.

If I couldn't decapitate this motherfucker with my teeth, I had other avenues.

I lunged, not waiting to get blindsided again, the blade piercing the delicate soft spot just under his chin. Luckily, the dagger was long enough to reach his brain. A twist of my wrist later, and I ripped it back out, settling in to saw his fucking head off before I asked Fiona to burn him to a crisp.

More and more arcaners filtered from the woods, my estimate of the numbers not nearly good enough.

We were more than surrounded.

We were overrun.

When a tall man with salt-and-pepper hair sauntered into the clearing, I knew exactly what this was. As his feral smile spread across his face, I realized that Belladonna, Paul's family—it had always been a trap.

And we'd walked right into it.

CHAPTER 19

FIONA

As soon as Theo told me we were being watched, I knew Josiah was in that forest somewhere.

The first time we'd walked through those trees, it had been as quiet as a graveyard. The animals and insects and even the wind itself were afraid of the apex predators walking through it.

But when we'd arrived tonight, even though Belladonna had poisoned an entire family, even though there was so much death, the forest had been alive with activity, hiding our footsteps, our movements. Why else would it be that loud if it weren't for Druids controlling the animals?

Why else would it be that loud, that active if it weren't cover for someone else?

It might have taken me a while to figure out it was a trap, but I sure as hell knew it now.

I watched Josiah saunter from the tree line, his slow gait as if he didn't have a care in the world. And the smile he wore on his stupid face, it was as if he had the entire universe in the palm of his hand, ready and willing to take hold of any and everything that he could possibly want.

What he didn't know was, that I held all of the power of the St. James annulet, that I was the St. James Coven leader. I'd done that on my own without him. Despite his efforts to pull me down, I had risen above.

No one was going to come after me for the explosion of this very house. No one was going to lock me up again.

Arcs of lightning rose from my fingers like ropes, slamming into the ground right at his feet. That made the smile finally fade from his lips. I wasn't going to be deterred by a bunch of rogue ABI agents and a witch who'd bitten off more than he could chew. And I sure as hell wasn't going to give him any of this power—not after what he'd done, not after who he'd killed.

"Well, Fiona, it's such a surprise to see you here." The sarcasm coming from his tone could choke a fucking goat. "I really wish you would have announced yourself. I would have fixed the place up."

"You mean after you destroyed it? After killing most

of your coven? Was that the plan all along, or did you decide on mass murder after I refused to do your bidding?"

That fucker had the gall to roll his eyes. "Oh, come on. Hendrick was a good lad. He would have made a decent husband—or his power would have at least been fine enough to steal. He didn't have to *stay* your husband."

"Is that the lie you tell yourself so you can sleep at night? I know what he planned to do as soon as that ring was on my finger. He planned to kill me. You're saying you knew nothing about that?"

A feigned expression of outrage lit his features, the falseness of it all turning my stomach.

"Of course not. Why would I send my only daughter off to be murdered?"

I was not chattel to be bargained or sold, and I sure as shit was not his daughter.

"Cut the shit, old man. I know I'm not your daughter, and I know what you did to my real family. Do you honestly think I'm going to let that stand?"

Flashbacks of June's torture ricocheted through my body. There was absolutely nothing he could say that would make me stand down, that would make me not want to watch his head roll.

Josiah's face hardened as his jaw clenched, and

through it all, he tried to ignore Theo moving from minion to minion, cutting them down one by one. Theo would protect me with his dying breath if he had to, but I didn't want that any more than I wanted to sit here and chew the fat with some lousy-ass motherfucker who killed my family.

"You will give me that annulet, Fiona. You will give me what I am owed." His sneer twisted his face. "You St. James witches, always trying to weasel out of a deal."

"Is that why you murdered my twin? Is that why you set her on fire?" Lightning slammed into the ground at his feet, making him stagger away. "Is that why you peeled the eyelids off my mother and made her watch her daughter get tortured?" Another bolt hit, this time closer, and he stumbled to the ground. "You think you're owed anything after that? Fuck you."

I raised my hands in the air, letting the power of the bloodline fill me—every cell, every molecule—it touched everything.

"You want this ring?" I asked, showing him my hand, the hammered golden circle on my right middle finger, exactly where June had always worn it. The same ring he'd ripped from her body right before he'd burned her alive. "Come and get it."

Josiah shot from the ground, the power he'd stolen far greater than I'd anticipated. Rising up, he floated several feet from the forest floor as thunder cracked in the air. All the tiny hairs on my arm rose, before a bolt of lightning bigger than I'd ever seen, slammed into the ground at my feet.

I went airborne, the forest tumbling in my vision as I catapulted into the dirt. Groaning, I picked myself up, not willing to be hit again. If he honestly believed that a single lightning bolt would end me, he had another thing coming. I found my feet, letting that power fill me once again, drawing on the coven, on the power gifted to me by the women who entrusted me to lead them. The same power that Josiah would steal the first chance he got. I didn't want to use their power. I wanted to use my own, but to stop him, I would do just about anything.

The earth trembled beneath my feet as a line of flames branched out from my every step, jumping from each blade of grass, seeking him out. He yelled out a war cry as he directed another bolt of lightning to me, but this one I caught. This one I absorbed. This one I took, ripping it from the very air. I held on to it as if it were a lifeline.

Smiling, I yanked on that bolt, pulling him to me.

Josiah wasn't a fan of hand-to-hand combat, hadn't thought it was important. As long as he'd been a witch, he'd never had to use it. Sure, he was lean and fit, preferring to take care of his body, but he never learned how to use the power of his fists, just like he never learned how to really be a witch. He was nothing better than a parasite, sucking up resources and power until there was nothing left.

Josiah thought he was the top dog, that everyone was trying to come after him. That everyone wanted what was his.

I didn't want what was his.

I wanted what was mine.

Letting my fist fly, I relished the crunch of his jaw cracking as my knuckles made contact. Making sure that behind that one hit, I put all the power he'd just thrown at me. He slammed into the trunk of a tree, his bones snapping as he struggled for breath.

But I'd gotten too confident. Cocky even, not expecting that when he was hurt, he would lash out with more power than I'd ever seen. A ball of flames hit me square in the chest, the heat of them stealing my very breath as they seared my skin.

A roar sounded from nearby, and it took me a second to realize it was Theo coming for me. But getting in the middle of us was too dangerous. Feebly, I tried to shove him away with my power, but even that was too much while I was still burning. Focusing on the flames, I drew them in, the worst of them dying out almost instantly. But still, my skin felt like it was on fire, the burns worming their way down my nose and throat, cutting off all my air.

But I would *not* let Josiah win.

One of the first spells I'd ever learned was from a nanny when I was five. I'd skinned my knee, and it was a bloody, dirty mess. She'd helped me learn how to heal myself, and with the power still under my flesh, I forced my skin to knit back together. Forced my air passages to right themselves, forced myself back on my own two feet.

Theo guarded my body, his white wolf pacing in front of me, snapping at anyone who got too close, his fur bloody, his back leg barely holding his weight. A vampire lunged at him, and luckily, Theo ripped him apart before I forced a shield up, separating us from them. Theo staggered back to me, his breaths just as heavy as mine.

And all the while Josiah laughed. His bloody smile spread wide as he taunted and jeered. And I wanted to fight—I did—but we were surrounded far more than we had been before.

I could choose to beat the man who raised me, but I couldn't do it without losing, too.

Glowing green eyes met mine, the knowledge passing between us. Theo knew we likely wouldn't make it out of there. In those eyes he was asking me if we should retreat, or if I wanted to fight it out to the end.

As much as my family deserved it, my revenge wasn't

worth losing him. It wasn't worth his life. It wasn't worth a long existence, aching for death as I passed the days without him. And I refused to let him spend his life back in that same hell—the hell of losing his mate. The hell of wishing for a death that wouldn't come.

But before I could say those words, a pair of golden eyes glowed in the darkness just inside the tree line. And then it wasn't just one pair of eyes.

It was two.

It was ten.

It was fifty.

Oh, so slowly, wolves stalked out of the forest, their growls giving Josiah's laughter pause. The LeBlanc pack had finally arrived. Behind those wolves stood a pissed-off Dahlia, followed by Hannah and Malia, Nico and Wren. And behind them all was a smiling Darby, her eyes alight with wrath.

Magic flew as wolves leapt for the circling ABI agents, their jaws going for the jugular as Wren and Darby raced for me, passing through my shield like it was nothing. My redheaded friend latched onto my arm, filling me with enough healing magic that I could breathe easy for the first time and what seemed like forever.

"We have to stop meeting like this," she muttered, wrapping her arms around me for a quick hug before turning to Theo.

Darby looked me over.

"I could have sworn that I told you to keep your nose out of trouble," she griped, snapping her fingers.

A mage that had been running right for us stumbled, his feet encased in earth as if the ground had come up to grab him. The earth traveled up his legs to his torso and then his head, encasing him until nothing but his nose and mouth were exposed.

Dirty agents ran, scattering like roaches after the light came on, trying to escape the onslaught of backup that had come to our aide. And while I wanted to give my thanks, wanted to tell them I appreciated everything they were doing for me, all I really wanted was to make sure Theo was okay.

Back on two legs, he lunged for me, wrapping me in his arms as he dropped a fierce kiss to my lips.

"Never again, Cupcake. We get through this, and we're done, you got me?"

Oh, I got him all right. I just needed to handle one more thing.

Holding his hand, I let out the power I'd been given, allowing it to fly like a heat-seeking missile. But it only had one goal in mind.

The thing that was funny and yet completely and utterly unsurprising? Josiah was running yet again, racing through the forest trying to get away.

From the pack.

From my friends.

From my family.

Lightning arced through the trees, and I relished the sound of his scream as my power wrapped around him, drawing him in one more time.

And as he drew closer, I realized the truth of it all.

I *could* kill him. I could watch his head roll. But he had to pay for his crimes. He had to be brought to justice—not just for me, but for every family that he'd wronged. Every person he'd stolen from. Every life he'd taken.

I imagined a pair of unbreakable cuffs surrounding his wrists, burning his skin. I imagined them at his elbows, around his shoulders, circling his waist, his thighs, his knees, his ankles, and with those cuffs, I trussed him up until he couldn't so much as move an inch.

Josiah screamed profanities, warning us that he would have his vengeance—or at least he did until I created another cuff to go over his stupid mouth.

I looked him straight in the eyes, the eyes that looked nothing like mine, and said the words that he'd avoided his whole life.

"Josiah Jacobs, you are under arrest."

And damn if that didn't feel good. He would go before

the council. He would be judged and executed, and his blood would never touch me again.

"Anyone got a phone? I need to call this in." Not that I really needed to. I was sure Sarina was in a car on her way to me right then, but I was leaving nothing to chance.

"I thought you handed in your badge," Darby quipped, the mirth shining in her eyes as she passed over her cell.

"Trust me, getting rid of it is at the tippy top of my to-do list."

Right after I made sure Josiah Jacobs would never breathe a day of free air ever again.

CHAPTER 20

FIONA

His trial lasted a whole week.

I didn't think it was possible for an arcane trial to last more than a few minutes, but that just went to show how insulated he had always been. How many favors he had stacked up. How corrupt my employer really was.

Several ABI agents had also gone down with him, everyone pointing fingers, trying to save their own skin as they attempted to explain away attacking one of their own at the behest of a kingpin. What was really fun was every single member of the LeBlanc pack had spoken to what they'd seen. Even Warden Adler herself provided damning testimony to what she had witnessed.

The other trials would soon follow, but until then, Josiah was in the hot seat.

I was just finishing up my testimony, highlighting the

murder of my family, my kidnapping, and the attack that had nearly taken my life. Most of the council was utterly exhausted, listening to every single person come forward to levy charges against Josiah, but I refused to feel one ounce of remorse. This was their job. If there was anything they were meant to do, it was to listen to the crimes of a man they had let walk free for far too long.

By the time I was done, I had nearly broken into a thousand pieces, reliving the hell that was my family's last hours.

But I had done it. For the family I lost and the future I could have had.

And when I was finished, Theo pulled me into his arms and whispered just how well I'd done, how proud of me he was. It took some of the sting away, but it didn't heal everything.

While I still had my badge, I'd gone to look in the archives. Not a single charge had been filed in the murder of my parents, of my sister. No one had even bothered to look for them. It was as if they had never existed, the ABI turning their backs on a coven without so much as a whisper of pause.

If I hadn't wanted to hand in my badge before, I sure as hell did then.

I couldn't work for people as corrupt as this, and this was coming from a mob princess. Josiah had rarely let me witness corruption to this degree, and yet, every second of my past felt dirty, wrong, like the stain of him would always be on me. It was possible I'd breathe easier once he was dead, but until then, I wasn't sure how I felt about myself.

"Is there anyone else?" Ingrid asked, her hands clasped in front of her, the most adult pose I'd seen her make yet.

It honored me that the council had listened to all of the testimony. I had a feeling Ingrid had a hand in that. Someone needed to listen. Someone needed to hear, and even if Josiah would never accept responsibility for the lives that he'd taken, it's still eased the burden on my heart to know others would learn of what he'd done.

When no one came forward, she gave a solemn nod and asked for the gallery to be cleared. All except myself, Theo, and Darby.

When we were finally alone, the small vampire met my gaze, her usually blue eyes red with wrath. Josiah was trussed up in the middle of the room, forced to listen to every murder, every sin, every crime, my cuffs binding him so that no one could release him.

He was covered in vomit, piss, and shit, unable to eat or drink. He was hanging on to life by a thread, the only thing to entertain him was the echo of every wrong he'd ever done.

"Remind me never to really piss you off," Ingrid said, staring at the pitiful figure of the man who raised me. "I'm pretty sure you could give Deimos a run for his money on the torture front."

I clutched a hand to my chest. "That's the nicest thing you've ever said to me," I joked, aiming for mirth, because the alternative would have me sobbing on the floor.

"You knew this would take a while when you petitioned for every witness you possibly could. You wanted him to hear it all before we killed him."

I shrugged. "I didn't think it was going to take seven fucking days, though. Which one of the council members does he still have in his pocket to extend his life like this?"

Ingrid just shook her head. "The extending part was to add to the torture, and you can thank Solana for that. She insisted on every witness being heard before he was put to death. Honestly, the two of you put together fucking frighten me."

I met the witch's stare, giving her a little finger wave before I returned my attention to Ingrid. "So, you will kill him, yes?"

"Honestly, I don't think any person in their right mind would keep him alive. For one, he has too much power under his skin from siphoning his whole coven. Keeping him in a null cell would backfire. Bad."

The testimony for the survivors had been horrific—worse when they found out it was their own leader who had done it. Though, I didn't quite understand how they were surprised. They knew far more about Josiah's exploits than I ever had.

"What am I doing here?" Darby asked. "No offense, I love learning all the tea. I'm just a little confused. Am I doing the executing here, or...?"

Ingrid's grin faded before she got down to business. "No, we're expanding your territory, Warden. You will now help police Tennessee and Kentucky. Before you ask, you will have a hand-picked team in several cities. And yes, we are looking to disband the Knoxville ABI. Again."

This wasn't exactly surprising. Sarina had done what she could, but there was too much corruption tainting the waters, and trust in the institution had long since fallen away.

Darby's face paled. "Not all the ABIs, right?"

Ingrid shook her head. "The ABI is here to stay, but the city of Knoxville and the list of agents now in our custody is too damning to recover from. The agents not picked up in the sweep will be forced to find other branches to take them, and the vetting process will now include truth serum."

I'd never been so happy to be handing in my badge. There was no way in hell that I would want a truth serum falling down my gullet. Then again, I was sort of surprised they hadn't been doing this already. But more than that, I was glad they were cleaning house, even if I wouldn't be a part of it anymore.

"We're about to call everyone back in, but that needed to be discussed."

"What discussion? You just made me Warden of two whole states instead of a single city." Darby's glare could have peeled paint. "I don't recall saying yes."

Ingrid planted her small fists on her hips. "You want someone else to have the job? By all means, name them."

Was it just me, or did that sound like a threat?

Darby narrowed her eyes at our tiny friend. "If I didn't know better—"

"But you do. You and I both know you are the only one we trust to do the job. You are the only one that I would trust to vet people appropriately, and don't tell anyone I told you, but having you as Warden has eased my mind about this city—about this region—far more than I ever expected."

"Oh, come on. Now I can't tell you no, you little shit," Darby grumbled, pinching her brow. "Fate told me it was supposed to be downhill from here. I can't see how getting more responsibility would make it downhill."

Ingrid slapped her back. "Delegate, my friend. Delegate."

When they recalled all of the witnesses into the gallery, my nerves hit me again. Theo must have felt it through the bond because he wrapped his arm around me and pulled me close, letting me know that he was there. That I could lean on him.

I knew this already.

Having Theo by my side had been the only way I could have made it through all of this. As the room filled, more familiar faces populated the crowd. The Acostas and the LeBlancs showed out in force. My coven, my family, Hannah, Malia, even my boss, Erica Serreno. Every one of them had come to help me through this.

The council called the room to order, a hush rippling through the crowd as they gave their verdict.

Solana stood, reading from a parchment like she was the foreperson of a jury.

"Josiah Jacobs, you are hereby charged with corruption, kidnapping, murder, endangerment of your coven, gross bodily harm, and a host of other charges—most of which I won't read to you because you've been convicted of all counts. In the history of the Arcane Council, not one defendant has stood trial for this long.

Your special circumstances are due to the fact that we wanted you to listen to every charge, to every testimony, so you knew what was waiting for you when you reached the Underworld."

I couldn't say whether or not I wanted to hear Josiah defend himself, but I never gave him the opportunity, deciding against removing his bonds, the testimony of so many proving his guilt hundreds of times over.

"As punishment for these crimes, you are hereby sentenced to death. Your sentence to be carried out immediately and witnessed by all your surviving victims."

A dark figure appeared in a wash of smoke, standing tall with a scythe in her hand, her wings spread wide for all the room to see. Her white hair was braided in a queue down her back, and the council bowed to her.

"Lady Death," Solana greeted, bowing low once again. "We implore you to please grant us this favor. This man carries too much power to be executed by our means. We wish that you carry out his sentence and take him with you to the Underworld."

Sloane gave her a wicked smile, her scythe at the ready. "The answer was already yes. And for future reference, I'm not like my father. I cannot be summoned. Any summoning you do is merely a request—one I can ignore at my leisure."

Solana took to her knees. "We will remember that, and you humble us with your assistance. We mean no disrespect."

Sloane's smile grew kinder, gentler. "She's coming home, you know. It won't be long now."

And with that cryptic statement, the Angel of Death turned to the crowd, gave us all a finger wave, and then took Josiah's head in one clean stroke. The power that had been trapped in his skin flew about the room, pieces of it breaking off from the mass that it had been and flowing into certain members of the crowd.

In killing him, Sloane had given them their power back. While everyone was marveling at the light show, I watched as she grabbed the soul of the man who raised me and disappeared in a wash of smoke, just like she had with Paul the week before.

But unlike Paul, Josiah was going to a very different place.

CHAPTER 21

THEO

SIX MONTHS LATER

I stared at my watch, trying not to grind my teeth. Today was special, and as usual, my brother and his wife were late to the party. A few members of the pack, Fiona's former boss, and a small contingent of Fae were all gathered in Chatham Square waiting for our pack to be whole again.

Today was the day.

It had been a rough and tumble six months, but we'd made it through, and now we were in the home stretch. Fiona had decided to set up a St. James Coven in Savannah, and trying to get that up and running had been a nightmare. But with the majority of the members residing in this state, it just made sense.

Plus, there was a considerable witch power vacuum here after the Fae doors closed that made the need to have a location in this city a better idea than most, especially when you considered most of the witches fled years ago. Slowly but surely, they were coming back, but the magic of this city was almost nil.

Fifteen minutes late, rumpled, and a teensy bit fuck drunk, my Alpha and his mate finally decided to join us. Luckily, nothing had come out of the gate yet, Wyatt and the motley crew also running behind. The Fae Queen, Áine, stood beside the door opposite us, her beatific smile unnerving as she stared at my wife like she was something she wanted to examine closer.

"Oh, good, right on time," Áine cooed, her smile not the least bit sarcastic. "I knew you'd be a little late today, so I padded the timeline a bit."

And that's not creepy or anything.

Three minutes later, the door that we'd been waiting six months to open creaked wide. Wyatt's blond head came out first, followed by a sea of women in various states of injury. Some walked of their own accord, and some were carried on makeshift stretchers. Tristan was the last one out, carrying a small woman with no hair and as thin as a rail.

Fiona's former boss whistled, and a team of medics descended, escorting them away so they could be attended to. After the last woman was handed off, Tristan's gaze landed on Mariella, the bond they shared not wavering in the least.

Fantastic. And totally not my problem. I couldn't change the bonds of Fate any more than they could.

Fiona moved toward the survivors from Faerie, the agents piling them into SUVs and ambulances to take them to be seen by healers. My wife's gaze locked on the bald one that Tristan had brought over, stopping the agents from pulling away, with a genuine smile and just a hint of sweetening. Fiona didn't use it often, the magic giving her a bad taste in her mouth, but she did when she had to.

"Natalia Pope?" she asked, her tone kind as she spoke to Solana's cousin. The frail woman nodded her head gratefully, but didn't say a word. What she did do was begin to sign. I could tell that she wasn't deaf, but it was completely possible that her vocal cords had been damaged. Or maybe the trauma had killed her voice outright.

I'd seen it happen before.

Fiona responded with sign of her own, speaking aloud as she did so.

"Your cousin sent me. She wanted me to make sure that you were okay, and let you know that she's on her way to pick you up—if that's what you want. I know you've been through a rough time, so I'll be brief. I wanted to offer you a place in my coven. I don't know if you would like to stay with the ABI, and much has changed in the years you've been gone, but if you wanted a spot, we would be happy to have you."

Natalia nodded gratefully, her signs speeding up, so even if I could understand, I was likely to be lost.

"We'll talk when you're better. Take your time to get settled, and we'll be here."

The St. James Coven had grown considerably over the past six months, and with it, Fiona's confidence had as well. She flourished with the new role, her desire to do good overruling any misgivings she might have had about herself.

She had shed the pain and the guilt of her former family, embracing it all like the magnificent woman she was.

I fit my arm over her shoulder, twirling a finger in her now-blonde hair. A part of me missed the purple, but I realized that Fiona wanted a tie to her twin and the features they shared. More than the power that ran through her veins, and more than the ring she turned on her finger. She needed to see her in the mirror, and truth be told, I didn't mind.

I grabbed her left hand, twirling the diamond on her

left ring finger before I kissed the mating mark on her wrist, directing her feet toward our home.

Fiona loved designer shoes and clothes and bags. What she also loved was sparkly rocks, and I had found the biggest, most ostentatious wedding set for my beautiful wife. Her mating mark was obvious enough, the bright glow impossible to hide, but I still loved that she wore my ring.

I still loved that she had my name.

And I would love this woman until the end of time.

Her hip bumped mine as she poked me in the belly, spinning on those death-defying heels as she walked backward.

"You getting mushy over there?" she teased, feeling my emotions through the bond as easily as I felt hers.

I grabbed her by the hand, reeling her back in, lifting her up so I could touch my lips to hers.

"When it comes to you, Cupcake? Always."

This concludes the Lost Witch Series.
Thank you so much for reading. I can't express just how much I loved writing Fiona & Theo and their ragtag bunch of friends.

If you would love to see a special glimpse of Fiona & Theo's *first meeting from HIS point of view, turn the page for an epic **Lost Witch Bonus Scene**. I hope you enjoy it!*

Want the skinny on future releases without having to follow me absolutely everywhere on social media?
Text "LEGION" to (844) 311-5791

BONUS SCENE

Dear Reader,

I hope you enjoyed The Lost Witch Series. Fiona & Theo have a very special place in my heart, and I am absolutely ecstatic for you to read more about her and her favorite wolf.

I have an extra special bonus scene for you as a thank you for reading. All you have to do is click the link below, sign up for my newsletter, and you'll get an email giving you access!

SIGN UP HERE:

https://geni.us/cc-bonus

Want more in the Arcane Souls World? Check out...

DEAD TO ME

Grave Talker Book One

Meet Darby. Coffee addict. Homicide detective. Oh, and she can see ghosts, too.

There are only three rules in Darby Adler's life.

One: Don't talk to the dead in front of the living.

Two: Stay off the Arcane Bureau of Investigation's radar.

Three: Don't forget rules one and two.

With a murderer desperate for Darby's attention and an ABI agent in town, things are about to get mighty interesting in Haunted Peak, TN.

Grab Dead to Me today!

run, choosing between a job and a bed or certain death sort of seems like a no-brainer.

If only there wasn't that silly rule about not killing people...

Grab Night Watch today!

Want more in the Arcane Souls World? Check out…

SPELLS & SLIP-UPS

The Wrong Witch Book One

I suck at witchcraft.

Coming from a long line of famous witches, I should be at the top of the heap. Problem is, if there's a spell cast anywhere near me, I'll somehow mess it up. As a probationary agent with the Arcane Bureau of Investigation, I have two choices: I can limp along and *maybe* pass myself off as a competent agent, or I can die.

Horribly.

Worse news? I seem to have a stalker in the form of a sinfully hot, perpetually grumpy wolf who seems to have a keen interest in keeping me alive.

Whose idea was this again?

Grab it now!

To stay up to date on all things Annie Anderson, get exclusive access to ARCs and giveaways, and be a member of a fun, positive, drama-free space, join The Legion!

facebook.com/groups/ThePhoenixLegion

Acknowledgments

A huge, honking thank you to Shawn, Barb, Jade, Angela, Heather, Kelly, and Erin. Thanks for all the things. You know what you did. Every single one of you rock and I couldn't have done it without you.

About the Author

Annie Anderson is the author of the international bestselling Rogue Ethereal series. A United States Air Force veteran, Annie pens fast-paced Urban Fantasy novels filled with strong, snarky heroines and a boatload of magic. When she takes a break from writing, she can be found binge-watching The Magicians, flirting with her husband, wrangling children, or bribing her cantankerous dogs to go on a walk.

To find out more about Annie and her books, visit www.annieande.com

facebook.com/AuthorAnnieAnderson

twitter.com/AnnieAnde

instagram.com/AnnieAnde

amazon.com/author/annieande

bookbub.com/authors/annie-anderson

goodreads.com/AnnieAnde

pinterest.com/annieande

tiktok.com/@authorannieanderson

patreon.com/annieanderson